Robin A. Lieberman
author of Searching for September

Published September 2022

Paperback ISBN: 979-8-9856298-5-9

Hardcover ISBN: 979-8-9856298-6-6

Library of Congress Control Number: 2022912608

For information address:
The Three Tomatoes Book Publishing
6 Soundview Rd.
Glen Cove, NY 11542
Web address: www.thethreetomatoespublishing.com

Cover Illustration: Samantha Rae Goodrich
Cover graphics and interior design: Susan Herbst
Author's Photo: Jen Harris

Dedicated to my children

Samantha Rae and Dean Spencer

*who have validated that my commitment to parenting has
been life's greatest journey that needs no destination.*

PROLOGUE

My Lily,

If you are reading this letter, please know that your mommy traveled to a very peaceful place. I've left our world because of the deep love that I have for you. There's so much to share and I hope you are old enough to understand why I'm not with you and Daddy. My life hasn't been easy and from the moment that you were a tiny seed growing in my belly, I've always wanted you to have a better life.

Giovanni and Antoinette Ricci, my parents, your nonno and nonna, raised me in a poor Italian town called Villacidro. My precious girl, they would have adored you! They became penniless shortly after I was born and could barely survive, no less manage a child to care for. Despite living far below the poverty level their fairy tale stories about a princess always opened the beginning of my day with bright hope. I was their princess, without the crown or castle.

An older, somewhat peculiar man named Piero was kind enough to give us food and shelter in exchange for my father working tirelessly in his fields while my mother performed all other duties in his small house. He was a very strict man and often mean-spirited to my parents but treated your mommy extra special. We lived with him for a lot of years until both my parents became ill and passed away. No longer a little girl and in my early teens, I was able to carry out some of the chores that I learned from watching and helping my mother. Your mommy still needed to survive.

Piero's house was always spotless, and my unskilled mother knew the basics of how to prepare food. Everything tasted so delicious. I was heartbroken when Piero would throw the food in the trash, call her a peasant, and tell us to not eat the meal. Hours later I would sift through his trash, remove the food that still looked edible, and secretly bring it to my parents' room. I cannot remember a moment when I wasn't hurting and broken, and when they died, I wanted to join them. Lily, you would have loved your nonni.

Having nowhere else to live and fearing the streets, I stayed with Piero. As I became a young woman Piero would often make me feel very uncomfortable and not allow me privacy in his home. Often, I would catch him watching me when I was showering or changing my clothes, and when I closed the door, he strictly enforced his rules that all doors in the house remain open at all times. When he realized I was showering in the middle of the night when he was asleep, he turned off the water before he went to bed.

Living with Piero became a nightmare, and when he commanded me to sleep in his bed, I packed the few things that

I had and left his house to survive on my own. I thanked the dear Lord that your nonna and nonno were no longer alive to witness Piero's disrespect.

After only a few days of begging for food I went back to Piero, but by that time he had another young girl living in his home and turned me away. Hungry with no place to go I survived by performing unrespectable deeds in the eyes of the law and God. The only way I could honor my parents' good name was to survive. Lily, I was an unfortunate girl who didn't choose my past and loved my parents so very much. Hunger got the better of me and no one should have to scour the streets for crumbs.

One afternoon, I remember sitting homeless by the side of a building in a less impoverished area. Three teenage boys passing by stopped to gape at me. One of the boys ate his sandwich as I watched, and I tried to imagine its taste and what it might feel like going into my distended belly. Saving just the crust he spat on the remains, then dropped it in my lap. The boys laughed and walked away, likely satisfied that they had their amusement for the day.

I tried to keep myself asleep, mostly to avoid the hunger pangs, and if I got lucky, then my dreams would provide me with food. It was much better to live in my dreams.

The day arrived when I was certain that death wasn't far behind. I needed nourishment and if my last ounce of energy wasn't used for survival then the sidewalk would claim my nameless body, dispose of the rags around me, and my soul would drift away with hopes to find my parents. I refused to succumb to life's unfortunate circumstances and all that my family worked for.

The trashcans became a haven for lost dreams, and find-

ing a wrinkled dress beneath a pile of discarded household items was my needle in the haystack. I washed in a gas station bathroom, put on the dress, pinched my cheeks hard for some color, and hoped that any man would pay me for a few moments of pleasure. I'd sometimes peek into Piero's bedroom when my father was working in the fields and watch him direct my mother on how to pleasure him. I'm doubtful that my father knew about this.

Being beautiful, just like my mother, I had some faith that I could attract men regardless of what I was wearing. If I weren't taken advantage of, which often I was, and paid for my services, I'd buy a cheap dress and a lip gloss to keep myself marketable. The remainder of my money was used for food.

The streets were harsh and aged me quickly. An abandoned car in a side alley became my shelter until I was pulled from it, half-asleep, early one morning. Lily, my Lily, in order to live I gave away my body but never my soul or my heart. The two were never connected because I would close my eyes and think about food. After being arrested for selling my body to the devil, Lucia Zezza, a spinster with no children of her own who knew of my parents, took me into her home and cared for me. She became my savior and guardian angel.

As my story continues, I met your father, Lucia's great-nephew, when he was visiting her. You must know that at the time I met your father I looked different than when I was found on the streets. Lucia cared for me and insisted that I live with her. She was lonely and valued my company, and in turn I was grateful because she became my only family.

Shortly thereafter, Lucia and I moved to Agerola and

started anew. Guilia, who became Lucia's closest friend and owned a small clothing shop, encouraged me to work. Guilia taught me how to greet customers and sell clothes and before long she was able to take a day off from work while I managed her store. While Lucia argued that she didn't want any of my earned salary I took pride in giving something back to the woman who saved my life.

When your father first saw me, he was captivated by my physical beauty, which, of course, I could never see in myself. My inner beauty was so simplistic because I was alive with food on the table and a place to sleep. Lucia has always been the true beauty, but I seemed to have charmed your daddy, a successful and handsome lawyer. He swept me off my feet and asked me to travel back to the states with him to get married. Lucia gave us her blessing, but deep down I felt great sadness leaving Lucia. And so our story with you, Lily, begins.

Understand that I didn't know your father well when we married because everything happened quickly. Lucia and I never spoke of my arrest and how I came to live with her. Lucia passed me off as Guilia's relative who needed a room to rent and there was no need to elaborate. I was respectable and worked hard to obliterate the girl who was found selling herself on the streets.

Years later your father learned of my arrest and let me know he was disgusted, calling me dirty and unworthy. Sharing my heart-wrenching past didn't seem to matter, and he angrily contacted Lucia demanding that she never speak of my past, angry with both of us for not disclosing the truth. By that time, I was pregnant with you and often wondered if that was the only reason he stayed with me. I was contin-

ually reminded of the lofty lifestyle he had provided, but I believe he married me for selfish reasons. A beautiful wife by his side would complete him and then he demanded that I attend college to round out his resume. What man of his caliber would have an uneducated street girl for a wife? My life with him over the years had been hell and I tried so hard to make him happy.

"An Italian woman who cannot cook," he would say. "What a joke."

In his cruel moments he would threaten to leave me, gain custody of you, and expose my past. It is important that you know the truth from me, and I hope that you become a woman of substance and kindness: traits passed down from mother to daughter, my love.

About a year ago your father took me to his firm's holiday event in Manhattan. The beautiful Blue Room is a private room in an upscale restaurant. As you can imagine, he dressed me up as his perfect doll but deep down inside it was all about "the show." No sooner did he and I walk in together than a stunning older woman approached us, and I extended my hand and introduced myself as his wife. Infuriated, she looked at your father and said, "You're married, you bastard? After all this time I find this out?"

I was devastated, and the one thing I was sure of is that your Dad could talk his way out of a paper bag. He is not an honorable man and Lily, for your sake, I tried my hardest to forgive him, but I've given up my self-respect. If I leave him, he will be sure I no longer have you. With all that I have suffered as a child and a young girl, I cannot suffer as an adult. I honestly don't know what is worse, being hungry for food or hungry for self-respect.

Lily, Daddy will always cherish you in a way he can never cherish me so I'm certain you will be more than okay.

Tonight, at The Beaumont Hotel, Mommy will be at peace. Your father will find me tranquil when he returns from the Blue Room, as I do not plan to go there again. Tonight, there will be no struggle or internal agony, only rainbows and waterfalls. In a luxurious bathtub in a candlelit bathroom, I will swallow a magic pill that will take me to a mystical place to dream.

Dream about you and your great Aunt Lucia, my lovely gems. Some of Mommy's most peaceful moments had to be in my dreams, and we will always be in each other's. I'll reunite with your nonna and nonno on the other side of the rainbow and bring them your picture. If I could live my life over again, I would live it the same way if it meant giving life to you, Lily Zezza, and I will go to sleep with that thought.

Your Mommy

CHAPTER 1

The Day Of

The weeping willows formed an exquisite canopy over the path to the altar, and the lush autumn foliage at its peak had created a Thomas Kinkade painting at its finest. White chairs with a large burlap bow lined the rows and the end of each aisle was dotted with a carved pumpkin sprouting similar autumn hues. The cedar-lined "Pond Room" boasted a glass ceiling and several asymmetrical windows offering a picturesque space to host the cocktail hour. This thirty-acre property backed up to a pond with two small waterfalls and was surrounded by several cozy treehouses for guests to experience an intimate moment. Treetop Forest, a wedding venue gem situated in central Connecticut, checked off all the boxes that would fulfill Lily's dream of a fairytale wedding at twilight. Lily was an only child with both parents deceased and I, September Webb, embraced her as one of my own after her father's untimely death. Teddy, Lily's father and my former lover, would not be resurrected to compromise the splendor of this sacred day.

Teddy, monster extraordinaire, squeezed the life out of all good things, then kicked them to the curb. He was buried without respect, leaving behind no legacy that held value. His soul traveled to a dark place, his demons in tow, and no heavenly courtesies would be extended. The word spread quickly that no angel should flutter to his corner of the dungeon.

It had taken several painstaking years for me to carefully unwrap his wrongdoing and usher Lily down a road to emotional freedom. I separated my own angst and disappointment from Lily's in an effort to help her grow strong without absorbing my venom. My own daughter, Sadie, and I had worked tirelessly this past year to create a wedding day that would look and feel like every young woman's fantasy. I was grateful that my relationship with Lily had always been supported, albeit the circumstances had been quite unusual. When Teddy abandoned me, my family also endured my pain. They coached me as I clawed my way rock by rock up from the abyss. It took serious soul searching to redefine my place in the world after Teddy, the thief of hearts, seduced me into his wonderland, then dropped me down a rabbit hole with my heart still yearning. Lily was just a child.

Sadie; her husband, Josh; and my son, Jack, had always been pillars of strength through my healing. Then Wesley Harlow stepped into my life. Cautiously optimistic, I allowed Wes to unpack his suitcase filled with decades of his own history. He effortlessly sketched himself into our family portrait, became my partner in crime, and found a way to recapture my badly bruised heart. It was shortly thereafter that Lily resurfaced and reunited with my family, and so the story continued.

Wes and I never officially tied the knot but had lived together, peacefully, for years. The three-carat oval diamond on my finger, bequeathed to me by my maternal grandmother, quelled the meddlers from further questioning. Wes, never having had children of his own, organically filled the boots of being a loving stepdad to all the children and considered himself a grandpa to Elle, Sadie, and Josh's daughter. Wes held the utmost respect for Sadie and Jack's natural father, whom they held in high regard. If Wes were given the green light, he would have added a wedding band to my finger, but throughout our journey I'd treasured the unquestionable stability of his love for me and never mused about next steps.

"Jesus, Sep, you nearly tripped over that cart with the wine glasses," Sadie muttered as she grabbed my upper arm and pulled me in close to her.

"Oh, my God. I still laugh when you call your mother by her first name," chortled Lily.

"And I call her G-Sep, for Grandma Sep. Don't forget about that!"

Elle, trailing behind us, didn't miss a beat! Heaven, please help us all if this little spitfire weren't involved in everything and anything. I took Elle's hand and all of us laughed!

Strangely, I don't feel like I'm old enough to have a daughter who is Sadie's age, no less a grandchild! I've kept my body toned for more years than I can count, and being "all legs" on a 5'10" stature makes a statement. I never appreciated my height until I reached adulthood. My emerald green eyes, which I inherited from my father, are the usual conversation piece, and the one asset that I love most.

Sadie, the product of two tall parents, did not inherit height. She's a size 2, 5'4" petite girl with a head of brown hair that's a showstopper! Sadie knows how to put it all together from head to toe. Her clothes are offbeat, some are "one of a kind," and fit her personality. She's very kind, very assertive, and very everything!

The event staff was scurrying about in their black uniforms to arrange the dinner seating for our ninety guests while the three of us tiptoed around them like we were walking through a land mine. Long tables queued down a manicured trail through the woods, and bamboo folding chairs were tucked under the ivory linen tablecloths with lace overlay. The bronze lanterns suspended from the trees would create an unparalleled ambiance when the sun retires.

Lily's guest list included immediate family, their colleagues from law school, and a sprinkling of some of my dearest friends. Sadie and Josh's close-knit group of friends, whom Lily and Adam were introduced to and sometimes gathered with, though a ten-year age gap stretched between them, would also be in attendance. We had become Lily's family a few years ago when we reconnected and selflessly gave her a sense of belonging and unconditional love. She had traveled an arduous road wrestling with her family's misfortunes. Lily freely expressed her needs and wants to me, as a daughter would to a mother, and I maintained open communication with Sadie, always sensitive to her thoughts.

Like Lily, Adam was an only child. With his father deceased and his mother living in Wisconsin, Adam had been added to the framework of our family. He was a gentle, unassuming, free spirit. I loved him from day one when Lily introduced us; she could not have chosen a better man as her "co-star! In many ways he reminded me of my son. Their personalities had countless similarities and when the guys were together, they behaved as brothers would. I was thrilled that Adam's mom would finally meet Jack.

Several years ago, Sadie and Josh's wedding was notably published in The New York Times. Lily tried to emulate Sadie in many ways. Anyone who knew Sadie agreed that she was a hard act to follow. Her beauty, brains, and finesse commanded the attention of a room filled with strangers with no introduction necessary. Sadie was tough as nails, and my granddaughter, who had just started full-day kindergarten, was no slouchy kid. As a first and only grandchild, Elle was the apple of everyone's eye with the sun rising and setting behind her. And Elle, like Sadie, had an opinion on everything.

Sadie, analytical as she was, had always been a cheerleader for Team Lily. Did Sadie pity her? Could it be that Sadie understood my pain after the demise of Teddy's and my relationship, thinking that if I kept a connection with Lily, it would keep me connected to Teddy? Quite frankly, I'd never asked myself that question.

Our immediate family would be lodging on the premises there at Treetop Forest. The duplex-style log cabins could only accommodate a few families and Wes insisted on footing the bill for our reservations, including Adam's mother's reservation. Sadie had pulled out all the stops and hired her well-established hairstylist, with her associate cosmetician, to turn us into runway models. It was costing Sadie a pretty penny and she refused to discuss splitting the bill.

"This is Lily's special day and I'm treating her like I would a sister. End of discussion, Sep," she said emphatically.

With only three hours until the ceremony, "us girls," including Elle, were assembled in Lily's cabin to get ready. Adam was imprisoned in Jack's cabin with Josh and Wes, no doubt imbibing Maker's Mark 46 on the rocks. Elle was quite the hostess, dancing around, and I assisted her in pouring champagne into plastic flutes.

"Here, Miss Lily Bride, this is for you. And here, Miss Mommy, this is for you. And, G-Sep, this is for you!"

She poured apple juice into her plastic flute and was clinking glasses with us every few minutes, without fail. Elle had also been given the important job of serving the petit fours sandwiches that Sadie had delivered from a pricey, and not so nearby, market. Sandwich wedges were delivered to the guys.

My head felt woozy from the champagne but I was so relaxed and allowing my mind to drift.

Sitting close to Lily, the conversation between her and the hair stylist grabbed my ear. "Danye, you are a true artist! My hair is beyond gorgeous and I'm sure having a thick mane makes it easy for you to style. I always loved the story of Rapunzel and you've recreated the hairstyle from the picture book."

"Yes, not everyone can carry this hairstyle."

"And aren't these the most beautiful pearl hairpins? Sadie found them on ETSY after scouring God knows how many websites!"

"They absolutely are, Lily," remarked Danye.

"Please be sure that my hairstyle remains unique when you're styling Sadie's hair," Lily requested. As the volume of her voice dropped to a whisper she added, "Sadie told me she bought hair extensions and I don't want her hair to be styled like mine. Maybe you can suggest a style that's simpler-looking? It's the bride's day to shine, right?"

"Oh, Lily, I wouldn't worry. Both of you will carry your hairstyles beautifully. I'll see what I can do."

Am I buzzed from the bubbly or is what I'm hearing a twinge of jealousy? I wondered.

Lily has an entirely different look than Sadie. Lily stands about 5'7", is big boned, and carries extra weight in her midsection, similar to her dad. Her face is cute, rather than pretty. Lily also has a brown mane, similar to Sadie's, and I can understand where there might be some competition.

When it was Sadie's turn to have her hair styled, I slowed down my drinking and watched Lily very closely. My Sadie never would have made a disparaging remark. Lily sat close by and watched Danye create a masterpiece for Sadie, a 1960's look. The extensions were added, and her hair was extra-long and full.

"Elly, sweetie, can you please bring Mommy the green cardboard box from the mini fridge?" Sadie requested.

"G-Sep, can you come with me?"

"Of course, Elle," I said, pulling myself off the chair.

Elle returned to Sadie with the small box and all of us were curious about its contents. "Mommy, can I open it?" she shrieked.

"Soon, Elly, soon." Sadie motioned for her to settle down.

Danye parted Sadie's hair straight down the middle and began weaving a French braid down the right side of her head. Last week Sadie had a double-process color with auburn highlights, paying handsomely for the extensions to be dyed the same color. Once the braids were secured at the bottom with a beaded elastic band, Sadie told Elle to open the box.

Elle pulled back the wax paper with her little fingers and the daintiest miniature sunflowers and orange gerbera daisies were uncovered.

"Oh, Mommy! Can I have them?" she pleaded.

"Danye is going to place them in my braids and if there are extra flowers, yes, you may have them. I promise."

The flowers were interwoven perfectly throughout the long braids and the finishing touch was a gold-beaded hippie headband found on a vintage website. We scoured the West Village, where she bought a burnt orange, fitted long dress with huge bell sleeves at The Psychedelic Pussycat. A knockout! My Woodstock beauty would be wearing matte gold platform go-go boots and, no doubt, beat to the tune of a different drum. Elle had a blast swinging from the wicker bubble chair and needed reprimanding several times from the store manager. We thought the fucking chair would fall off the ceiling hook! Elle had adopted our love for the "flower power" era. Sadie was dressing her in an orange, A-line, tea-length dress with a '60s flower sash, made to order. It was shocking that she had found child-size go-go boots at a local thrift shop.

"Sadie, oh, my God, your hair looks amazing! How did you dream that up? Seriously? It's the coolest look ever and all eyes will be on you," Lily announced loudly.

"Thanks. Sep and I are hippie freaks and this is our trademark, so to speak. Wait until you see your flower girl. Elly got into the mix, too!" said Sadie.

"Elle, come to G-Sep," I instructed. "I have something special for you."

"A present? For me? I love getting presents!" Elle clapped her hands.

"This, Elle, has been in the family for years. Your great-grandma bought it for me to wear on my wedding day, and your mommy also wore it when she married Daddy. As the flower girl, I would like you to wear it."

"I'm the flower-power girl, remember?"

Elle hovered over me as I opened the velvet pouch and removed the rhinestone tiara.

"Oh, G-Sep, this is for a princess! Just like in the movies where all the princesses have crowns. Can I keep it?"

"That's so beautiful, Elle," Lily exaggerated. "Do you want to see how it looks on my head?"

"You can try it on, but I get to wear the princess crown today!"

"Well, of course you will," Lily assured as she gently positioned it on her head. I observed Elle's smile turn into a scowl. She watched Lily carefully adjust the tiara on her head and admire herself in the mirror. Elle fidgeted impatiently, her fingers crunching the fabric on her robe. I knew my granddaughter well; she wanted the tiara back in her little hands and was holding back a growl.

After some awkward hesitation Lily removed the tiara, placed it on Elle's head, and said, "You're one lucky little girl."

CHAPTER 2

A Walk Down the Aisle

A colossal treehouse with a winding wooden staircase and carved banister would reunite Lily with Adam when she elegantly descended to the flutist playing, "We've Only Just Begun." This weekend's Indian summer had overpowered the autumn weather, allowing us to leave behind our wraps and shrugs.

There was no large wedding party. Adam asked Josh to be his best man, and Sadie was the matron of honor. Elle, the "flower-power girl," would deliver stems of orange gerbera daisies from an antique watering can to the congregants. Lily would follow behind Elle, and once Lily reached the bottom of the treehouse I would escort her toward the altar, where Adam would receive her.

The theme for the wedding, given the venue and season, was creative and formal. Sadie's idea, of course, which Lily approved. Some of the men were wearing suits with autumn print ties and pocket squares. The women had become imaginative and were matching dressy bustiers with floral-print skirts. One guest was wearing culottes with a feathered halter. It was very much a fairytale wedding.

The flutist began and the chatter in the rows faded to silence. At the top of the treehouse Sadie appeared, holding large, thick stems of sunflowers wrapped in burlap and gold cord. She was exquisite and I watched Josh's expression; no man could have loved her more. Sadie reached the bottom of the stairs, walked to the altar, and she and Josh stood together. They watched their Elly come down the stairs, proudly wearing her tiara, atop a mound of curls, like she was just crowned Ms. Universe.

"Here, G-Sep, a daisy for you." I was her first recipient.

"Thank you, precious girl. Now give some of the daisies to the guests."

Elle distributed the daisies to those sitting on the aisle seats and then stood between her parents.

"Oohs" and "Aahs" filled the air when Lily emerged, her gown a simple white and blush two-tone strapless with a full-beaded sweetheart top. The bodice was fitted with plain tulle flowing from the waistline to the floor, and as she walked down the stairs, the small sweep on the back of her gown bounced off each step. Her tussie-mussie, a Victorian-style bouquet with white roses and lavender, was carried in a fluted nickel holder. Lily reached the bottom of the staircase, and my eyes accumulated enough tears to blur my vision.

"How do I look, Mom?"

Lily had never called me "mom," and in that moment I recognized the enormity of my place in her life.

Looking up to the heavens I prayed that Tessa, Lily's mother, was here with us. It was a privilege to be standing in her shoes, but the feeling was bittersweet.

"I love you, Lily," I replied. "Your family is here, some in spirit. Let's do this thing, shall we?"

The buckets in the bottom of her eyes were beginning to spill over with tears of joy. "Hold my hand, Mom?"

I held out my hand and proudly walked her down the path. Adam met us halfway, and once joined, I lifted her veil and kissed each of her cheeks.

"Love you, Seppie," Adam said and hugged me.

Their hands interlocked and they strolled to the altar. I found my seat next to Wes.

"Beautiful," remarked Wes. "Absolutely beautiful."

I turned to Wes.

"Yes, you, Seppie, my love."

The ceremony began. Elle left her parents' sides and ran to Wes and me while holding her tiara in place.

"G-Sep, G-Sep, I want to sit with you," she yelled.

"Shh ... okay, but the ceremony has begun, and we have to be very quiet," I whispered. Wes pulled Elle up on his lap and she handed me the tiara. I was distracted watching Wes with Elle, who had no children or grandchildren of his own. I had given Wes and Lily a family and sometimes took my blessings for granted.

The officiant performed their rite of passage into holy matrimony, which proved to be an emotionally moving experience. Lily was raised Roman Catholic and Adam was Jewish. The officiant's speech was not delivered as a homily but as a message of importance to build a loving, mutually respectful, and peaceful home. He added a personal touch when describing the circumstances of how they first met and their growth from friendship to lifelong partners. Lily's unsettled past had been anything but peaceful and I was warmed to the core that this chapter of her life had stability. Lily and Adam had bridged all their holidays and my family participated in Lily's traditions. The officiant spent a significant amount of time getting to know them to preside over a ceremony that represented their individuality and who they had become as a couple.

"Oh, G-Sep, I want to get married, too!" Elle said loudly. "I will marry either Daddy, or Adam, or Uncle Jack!"

"Silly girl," I said with an exaggerated look of surprise, "it doesn't happen that way!"

Elle leaned back into Wes and crossed her arms across her chest with a pouty face.

I watched her, then said, "Elle, Mommy and I will have to explain to you how this wedding thing works, yes?"

"Well, okay, I guess," she puffed back.

At the conclusion of the ceremony Elle bounced off Wes' lap and started collecting the daisies that dropped on the ground. Guests who were still holding their daisies placed them back in her watering can as she walked by.

"I'd like to say a few words before all of us make our way to the Pond Room," Lily announced on the microphone.

Elle ran back into the aisle with us.

"My heart is bursting with joy," Lily continued. "Adam and I are privileged to have found each other and thankful for the abundance of love from everyone supporting us on our wedding day and every day. I am blessed that Seppie adopted me into her wonderful family after losing my parents to unfortunate circumstances."

Lily reached out and took Adam's hand in hers.

"Seppie once spoke to me about gardens, a conversation

I've always held close to my heart. She said that when we mature and make our way into the world, we grow a garden of our own. The family garden, however, will always be there to visit. Adam and I will now tend our own and I'm grateful for the seeds that Seppie has given me over the years. I often think about the lineage that connects Seppie, Sadie, and Elle, something so natural and special. When I was thinking about a gift of acknowledgment that I could present to them on my wedding day, I asked my jeweler to design a gold four-leaf clover. He sectioned the clover into four pieces, created a charm, and attached it to a gold charm bracelet that each of us can fill over the years."

"Oh, G-Sep, more presents!" Elle said, hugging my neck.

"I hope," Lily continued, "that our bracelets keep us close and in good health because there is so much more to come. Elle, would you like to come up and bring the bracelets to Mommy and G-Sep?"

"Yes, and a bracelet for me!" Elle almost fell down, face first, as she rushed to get out of the aisle to make her way to Lily to grab those pouches.

Lily handed her three velvet pouches and Elle proudly brought them to us.

Adam took the microphone from Lily. "Thank you, everyone, for celebrating with us in this magical forest. Tiger Lily is my special gift and the greatest gift all of us can give each other is to cherish what we have in the moment."

Adam lifted his arm while holding Lily's hand and shouted, "Let's party!" I'd always adored Adam's nickname for her—Tiger Lily!

As our guests filed out of the rows, Sadie, Elle, and I waited together to thank Lily for her gift. It crossed my mind that

Sadie might view Lily's gift as a way to ingratiate herself into our lineage. Even if Lily had asked for my opinion about this gift prior, it would have been awkward for me to suggest something different. To Elle, it was another present. To Sadie, well, I believed Sadie was secure enough to acknowledge this as a heartfelt gesture. I didn't plan to share my thoughts and would accept this gift as her deep appreciation for where my family had carried her—over rough terrain, indeed.

"Lily," Adam called out, "let's make our way to the cocktail hour so we can greet our guests."

"Be there in a sec, Adam," she said as she noticed the three of us approaching her. "Oh, Lily, these bracelets are beautiful and heartfelt and ...," I began to say.

"More presents, Lily Bride!" demanded Elle.

"Oh, Elly, really?" scolded Sadie. "Lily, so thoughtful. Can us girls do a group hug?" We snuggled in tight.

"I'm ecstatic that you love my gift and on special occasions we can add charms." Lily looked past us. "Oh, Adam, coming now," she called out while waving her hand. "Adam is waiting to walk in with me. Love you all!" Lily went to join Adam.

Josh walked over to Sadie, and when they tried to take Elle's hand, she snuggled next to me.

"Wes and I can bring her into the Pond Room," I suggested. "The two of you head on over?"

It took us a while to move Elle along to the cocktail hour. She found it necessary to talk to the pumpkins at the end of each row, giving each one a name. "You're Daddy, and you're Adam, and you're my Uncle Jack," smiled Elle. One pumpkin was the target of her aggression.

"No," shouted Elle, "I won't marry you!"

"Okay, Elle," I said sternly, "enough of this! We need to go now." Wes and I latched onto each one of her hands and began our trek to the next destination. Elle looked back at the pumpkins as we dragged her away, her shoes barely touching the ground. All the while she pursued her line of questioning.

"Who can I marry, G-Sep? When can we talk to Mommy about who I can marry? I want to have a wedding right away. This is so much fun!"

"Elly, there you are," said Sadie, exiting from the Pond Room. "Daddy and I want to introduce you to someone."

"Sadie, Elle is trying to plan her wedding and we'll have to explain to her why she can't marry Daddy, Adam, or Uncle Jack," I told her.

Sadie tilted her head and peered intently at Elle. "You're not serious, Elly?"

"It doesn't work that way," Sadie and I said in unison, then laughed!

"Elly, honey, Mommy will explain this to you later. Come with me," she insisted, taking her hand and tugging her away.

"My daughter has her work cut out for her." I turned to Wes.

"Well, Seppie, she could marry me. After all, I am available, right?" Wes intimated with seriousness of purpose and a stoic look.

He held his stare, sending a shiver down my spine, as if waiting for my reply to a marriage proposal.

His elbow fanned outward while he held his gaze, and I looped my arm through his to escort me into the party.

"Shall we make our way to the cocktail hour?" I suggested.

"Indeed."

That day, the stars were aligned. Cooperation from the weatherman and everyone arriving safely set the stage. The

Pond Room looked magical! When we entered, the guests swarmed around us to give their heartfelt congratulations. I had stepped in as the mother of the bride. And Wes? Well, Wes was just Wes, always relaxed and following my lead. We complemented each other in so many ways; a perfect fit, a solid team.

"You're sexy as hell," he whispered in my ear. "I want you to walk over to the bar and order us drinks."

"Oh, really, boss man?"

"Yes, Seppie, do as you're told. I want to watch you walk over there ... and walk slowly."

Of course, I knew where he was going with this. I was wearing something suggestive and untraditional, a "Sadie a la mode." The more I thought about it, the more I could not believe she'd convinced me to buy that dress. It covered my body completely up to my neck and was slightly fitted to the floor and long-sleeved in a goldenrod color. The dress was completely backless, dipping low, just above the crack in my ass. No panties necessary and I was wearing "cutlets" that held up my breasts. Sadie added a long, gold Y necklace with citrine stones and Swarovski crystal that hung all the way down my back. The little wiggle in my walk in my gold Stuart Weitzman sling backs set Wes on fire!

There's something I find to be very sexy when approaching a bar to order a cocktail. Mostly men surrounded this grandiose, mahogany bar, and I became a distraction.

"Good evening, sir. May I have champagne and Makers on the rocks?"

"Of course," he said with a smile, and a stare that lasted a few seconds longer than it should have.

The bartender, tall and fit, had a boyish look with a long

lock of hair brushed to one side. His eyes studied me, in that brief moment, and damn I know I look good.

Once served, I turned to walk back to Wes, who hadn't moved. Wes is broad shouldered and ruggedly handsome with reddish highlight to his hair. His height allows me to comfortably wear high heels and still look up to him, and he and I have a presence when we enter a room.

Wes was standing with his hands clasped in front of him, watching me. I could tell he was in one of his crazy moods.

"Oh, girl, you carry it well. I'll take the drinks, and you follow me out of here," he said.

"Follow ... What? Follow you where?"

"We're going to hit up one of the treehouses. Please. Amuse me," he insisted.

Earlier, he and the guys must have consumed quite a few drinks while they were getting dressed, and I could smell the alcohol on his breath. It drove me batshit crazy in a good way, and he knew it. I thought back to that scene from the movie *Carrie* when Piper Laurie said to Sissy Spacek, "I smelled the whiskey on his breath. Then he took me. He took me, with the stink of filthy roadhouse whiskey on his breath, and I liked it. I liked it!"

Holy crap, fuck the damn treehouse! Wes should just hoist up my dress in the woods and bend me over a fallen bough! We were untraditional in that way.

He and I surreptitiously wormed our way out of the Pond Room for a few moments of seclusion.

The sun was beginning to close its eyes and I glanced back toward the Pond Room; the lights were now on a dimmer.

Wes shepherded me to the treehouse farthest from the Pond Room where a plastic "RESERVED" sign hung from a hook nailed into the wood.

"You snake!" I scolded. "Is this your crafty work?"

"I'm afraid it is," he replied in a childish voice, looking sheepish and hanging his head low.

"What am I going to do with you?"

"You tell me," he replied, engaging me with his stare.

Wes placed the drinks inside the treehouse first so that he could help me step inside. A man on a mission! He then extinguished the light in the lantern hanging outside of the treehouse, no doubt to deflect any attention. There were still traces of light coming in, so we weren't in complete darkness. As I grabbed onto the wood rail, I felt the warmth of Wes' palms underneath my buttocks. He squeezed them gently while lifting me up.

"Jesus, Wes, these heels are taking a beating!"

"Your ass should take a beating," he laughed. "Quit your bitchin', girl."

Once inside, I found a red and black tartan blanket that I recognized from our room. That sly fox had thought of everything.

He spread out the blanket and then commissioned me to sit on his lap. As I moved around to get comfortable, I could feel his arousal.

"Lift up your dress, then turn around and face me," he commanded in a low, seductive voice.

I removed my heels, placed them on the bench, and then stood up to lift up my dress. Wearing no panties made it effortless to comply. While he unbuckled his pants and allowed them to drop around his ankles, I guzzled the remainder of my champagne like a sailor. He introduced his already hard penis through the opening on his briefs and I took my position, facing him while guiding him inside me.

Oh, so warm and inviting. It was always good with him. He was gentle and unassuming. I was turned on that, though he said less than most, I could read so much more behind so few words. "Look at me, Seppie," he murmured as he moved my buttocks back and forth rhythmically. I looked down at him, my braids brushing the sides of his face.

"I'm waiting for you, Seppie." And I heard the struggle in his tone while slowing the back-and-forth motion.

"Love, there's no need to slow us down. Kiss me now. I'm there."

My thought of someone finding us screwing like feral children was what brought me over the threshold to peak, and then our bodies trembled in the safe harbor of each other's arms.

We held each other tightly while the waves of our orgasm rolled back to ripples, my face tucked comfortably in the crook of his neck.

And as the darkness closed in around the treehouse he whispered in my ear, "Marry me, Seppie."

C H A P T E R 3

Post Wedding Recovery

Lily and Adam escaped to the Hotel Byblos Saint-Tropez, on the French Riviera, for an eleven-day honeymoon. Lily, a sun worshiper, often sang the song from the once-popular Bain de Soleil sunscreen television commercial, "Bain de Soleil for that Saint-Tropez tan." She indulged in everything French like Chanel parfum, dining in bistros, and picking up delicate flower bouquets from Boulangerie et Bouquets, a pricey corner market. Oh, she loved her French mani/pedis, I might add, and simply had a fascination with anything Français! Although born of pure Italian descent, she was drawn to the romance of the French.

Sadie and I assisted Adam in the planning of special honeymoon events to surprise her. They would be spending one of their mornings in a couple's cooking class baking croissants, and for them that was surely something extraordinarily different. On another day they were booked for a cycling tour that included an elaborate picnic with wine tasting. As part of their wedding gift, Sadie and I assembled Lily's wedding trousseau to include provocative lingerie and other personal items ... the "must-haves," and everything French! Their honeymoon was a welcomed break, affording me time with Sadie for desperately needed rest and relaxation. She and I had been the foot soldiers throughout the wedding planning, which required enormous mental and physical energy. During that honeymoon period Sadie requested a few days off from work to be with Elle and me. I often felt pulled in different directions, and perhaps that was because I'd "adopted" another daughter.

We were booked for a morning at a nativity spa in the Flatiron District, inspired by the tradition of the baths from ancient Greek and Roman civilizations. The spa, which we had visited for the first time a week prior to Sadie's wedding day, was located in a renovated historical building.

Clientele were completely immersed in the ancient atmosphere of their underground walkways. Lanterns were strategically placed along the guest's journey, creating ambiance and the feel of seclusion. The entire space was designed to look like ruins, and the sensation of submerging one's body in a variety of temperature baths pulled you from the hustle and bustle of city life. That $400-per-person journey was our "special occasion go-to place," which included a thirty-minute massage and complementary health bar.

Wes and Josh put their heads together and reserved, for the following day, a "girls' night" at the St. Regis, dinner and cocktails at their King Cole Bar, and an overnight stay in one of the suites. The guys would entertain themselves at home with a movie-and-pizza night, Elle included, and had enlisted

Jack to join the fun. While the guys enjoyed a beer night, there would be lots of sugary drinks for Elle, which would keep her bouncing off the walls. Sadie and Josh were very health-conscious with her but would occasionally allow her the luxury of junk food consumption so she didn't constantly bark for it.

On the day of our overnight, Sadie and I separately hailed taxis to the St. Regis and found each other at the reception desk slightly before the 3 p.m. check-in. Our rolling suitcases were filled with enough clothes to last us for a week! Our plan was to use their fitness club shower, get gussied up, and head downstairs to the King Cole.

When we opened the door to our suite a chilled bottle of Perrier-Jouet was waiting for us, alongside chocolate-dipped fruit slices, compliments of our men. The note card on the table read: "Enjoy the evening, ladies! With love from Josh and Wes (future husband)"

Wes was over the moon about my accepting his marriage proposal. For so many reasons I believed that second marriages struggled to survive, but our journey had been seamless and uncomplicated. He had been my husband without the title. As Sadie said, "It's about damn time, woman!" The children had been ecstatic since hearing the news of our engagement.

"Let's unpack, Sep!" said Sadie.

We began pulling our clothes from the suitcases. I didn't remove items that were complimentary from the hotel like soap, hair products, and my hairdryer. Preparing myself for a hardy workout, I began squeezing into my tights and sports bra. But no sooner had I laced up my sneakers than getting to the health club became a fleeting thought and was no longer a choice.

"Sep, this is superb! Josh and Wes are quite the team. Crack open that bottle, bitch, and let our girls' night begin!"

For years Sadie had called me "her bitch." A somewhat endearing term, so she told me. What could I say? I raised a Brooklyn beauty!

"Indeed," I agreed. "I don't think we're making it to the gym after two glasses. We'll drink and bullshit and then get ready. Our reservation is set for seven."

We sipped champagne from the etched flutes and mused about the details of the wedding.

"Sadie, do you think Lily was upset that I didn't offer the tiara to her on her wedding day?" I asked.

"What would make you ask me that question?"

"Well, it's the way she toyed with it on her head. I found that to be an awkward moment for Elle."

"I suppose so. Quite frankly, if Lily held onto that tiara a minute longer Elly would have kicked her in the fucking shin! Sep, I mean, I love Lily and all but ... Elly's tiara? Really? My Elly?"

"Jesus, poor Elle must have been sweating like a gypsy with a mortgage!" I laughed.

"Sep, you're drunk. Slow down the drinking!"

"C'mon, don't be a shit-stirrer, although I was thinking the same thing. I don't know, maybe I should have offered it to Lily. She's been a part of our family, views you as a sister and me as a mother figure, and wow, the bracelets that she designed for us! Having lineage is important to her. Perhaps we should have had the conversation ahead of time, but the day has come and gone. Enough of this talk about the tiara."

My girl and I were getting ready like it was prom night, the bathroom counter littered with makeup, brushes, face cream, you name it. Laughing, gossiping, styling our hair, gossiping, well … a lot of gossiping because that was just what we did. Elle had called us several times to say hello and the tenor of her voice sounded forlorn. After the fifth phone call I knew the hatchet was about to descend.

As one might have imagined, Elle fussed and fussed, and Josh had to bring her to the hotel room to sleep with us. It wasn't that she gave a shit about being with her mom and her G-Sep; she was more interested in living out her fantasy as the pampered little princess that she was. We were summoned to run a jacuzzi bath for her after requesting more bubble bath from housekeeping because Elle refused to take the samples out of her overnight bag. Most of the items that weren't nailed down she hid from us within the first ten minutes of arriving at the room.

Elle refused to change out of her clothes to get ready for her bath, and we already knew the requirements. Until there were bubbles floating twelve inches above the tub, the bath was not yet worthy for her highness! However, once the drawing of the bath met her expectations, we had the sheer pleasure of witnessing Elle's grand carpet entrance to the evening's premiere. Without exaggeration, the kid flung open the sliding doors from the walk-in closet and made her debut. Dressed head-to-toe in an adult-size white waffle robe with hotel logo embroidery, slippers to match, and Sadie's big-ass Prada sunglasses, she strutted toward the tub with her queen bee attitude and way too much fabric trailing behind her.

She relaxed in that tub like the Queen of Sheba, eating the chocolate-covered fruit, until she looked like a prune. The evening became "all about Elle," but Sadie finally put her foot down when she attempted to access the mini fridge. It was a generational rule. No one in the history of our family had ever been allowed to touch a mini fridge in any hotel room. Dating back to my childhood and then passing down that directive to my children, it was strictly enforced. The warning was delivered before the start of a vacation with the threat of broken fingers if we were caught within two feet of the fridge. Spending eight dollars to consume a Milky Way bar that cost a dollar was unfathomable. Now feeling badly that Elle had been reprimanded I allowed her to choose one item.

"Elle, honey, you can pick out one treat. Anything that you want."

Sadie looked my way and gave me an eyeball roll, accompanied by a nod of approval. The little princess couldn't possibly comprehend what the commotion was about. She simply opened a dollhouse-size refrigerator and the shit had hit the fucking fan! "Can I, G-Sep?" she asked sheepishly.

"Yes, you may."

She reached in and kept touching both the M&M's and the small can of Pringles, but when she looked back at me and I frowned, she snatched the M&M's.

Sadie ran her household differently and likely believed that most of my "no-no's" were outdated. She didn't feel the need to carry those old seeds into her nest. There were a few rules, though, that she followed in my presence out of respect for how I raised her. When she and I dined out I almost always refused a glass of wine. It seemed ludicrous to pay the price for a glass of wine that cost the same as the entire bottle at a liquor store. But Sadie was relentless, a sergeant! She didn't hold back and reminded me how much I deserved that glass of wine, reinforcing that it was our special time to live in the moment.

Her significant level of business travel commanded that she wind down after a grueling day of meetings. She'd pluck the most expensive bottle of wine from the mini bar and run a bath. Sophisticated Sadie never felt undeserving and was an absolute master of deterring others from renting space in her head. She'd worked herself ragged to climb the corporate ladder to success and exuded confidence, knowing exactly what she wanted for herself and what was best for her clients, a creative visionary in high heels with high ambitions. I swear, she could have sold bagged dogshit, and people would have lined up and cleared the shelves!

Well, you guessed it; Sadie and I never made it to the King Cole. We ordered room service, which cost a small fortune, then wandered out to find the nearest Pinkberry for ice cream.

CHAPTER 4

The Honeymoon is Over

The newlyweds were scheduled to return home late that evening. Since they gave me a spare key to water the plants and check on their apartment, I made a few "light shopping" purchases at Whole Foods for the basics to tide them over until they could go grocery shopping. With the apartment closed up, staleness hung around like an unwanted guest. Pulling back the curtains and opening the windows, I welcomed the crisp October air to breathe life into the rooms. The chrysanthemums that I grabbed at checkout needed a vase, so once the groceries were put away, I decided to hunt down a vase or large jar. A special touch so their honeymoon could continue after they opened their front door.

Their kitchen cabinets were meticulously organized to make the most of the small space that they had to work with. I began opening the bottom cabinets, holding out some hope of finding a vase. After having zero luck, I used the step stool, which allowed me to check the larger cabinets above the sink where those items would typically be stored. Alas, three large Mason jars were staring right at me. Balanced on top of the jars was a collection of French recipe books. My little French girl! Carefully, I removed the books and a jar.

I was not one to collect cookbooks, like Sadie and Lily, but preferred googling online recipes if I needed one. Amongst the books was something that resembled an album, and I was thinking that maybe she saved written recipes in a separate type of scrapbook. She likely had saved my blintze recipe, which had always been her favorite. I was also curious if there were any Italian recipes that she saved from Teddy. I figured that ought to be interesting and there was no harm in peeking. For Christ's sake, it was not the same as rummaging through her panty drawer or opening her medicine cabinet.

I filled the jar with cool water and dissolved the contents in the small packet of Floralife before arranging the yellow flowers. After wiping the wetness from the bottom of the jar I set it down on the table and perched myself on their sofa to look through what I thought would be her recipe book.

On the first page of the album was a clipping she found from Sadie and Josh's wedding. What the actual fuck? I had once mentioned to her that the *Sunday Styles* section of *The New York Times* published an article on their wedding venue, which included an interview about how they met. Their wedding picture accompanied the write-up and had become quite the buzz. Phones were blowing up! She must have searched for that article and printed it. In red ink, where Sadie's and Josh's names appear, she placed a line through it and added her and Adam's names. Unequivocally, Lily had always tried to emulate Sadie, but finding this was disturbing.

Apprehensively, I turned the page and saw two pictures of Elle, who could not have been more than two years old when they were taken. They looked like cellphone pictures that had been saved to an email and printed. Above the pictures, written in red ink: "Our Precious Baby Elle." Beneath the pictures was a small clipping of hair in a snack-size Ziploc that was taped to the page. *How the fuck did she do this?* I wondered. *Was she ever alone with Elle to cut a snip of her hair? Did Adam know about this album? Should I take pictures of this and show them to Wes and Sadie?*

My body went numb, and nausea rolled like waves in the pit of my stomach. *Holy crap, this is no joke!*

The pages that followed held several keepsakes and among them was a crushed, dried purple tulip that I believed was from several years ago when I brought them to my first visit to their apartment. The following page was left blank, but the next page displayed a magazine cutout of some "hippie chick." Taped next to it, a miniature wilted sunflower. In blue ink, written underneath the picture: "I wish this were me."

That sunflower was surely from Lily's wedding; one of the ones weaved through Sadie's hair. Lily had a forty-eight-hour turnaround time to add this to the album before leaving for Saint-Tropez. The hippie picture was a clear declaration of Lily's jealousy of Sadie. Sadie, stealing her thunder by the very virtue of who she was. Sadie, with all her selfless acts of kindness and good intentions, was being targeted because jealousy was rearing its ugly head and wanted to be in control. This felt like Teddy's relationship with me and his need to control. The parallel was worrisome as I remembered being in a position where giving your very best was never good enough for the other person.

Dizzy with confusion and disappointment, I felt out of my element. My body memory had stored a lot of the trauma from years spent with Teddy and was reacting to this discovery in a similar fashion. Heartbroken, I was alone with these thoughts and didn't know where to carry them. I knew with certainty, Lily was struggling with her position in our family. Was she creating this imaginary life where she had me as her mother while secretly wishing Sadie would vanish? My Sadie appeared to glide around the universe, collecting all of life's great moments with Sep by her side. We were two peas in a pod, best friends and a mother-and-daughter team, yet we had always made room for a third pea, Lily, whom I had always called my "sweet pea."

It was mind-boggling, difficult to wrap my head around, because I had always given and continued to give Lily an overabundance of love and attention as did the rest of my family. The preparation for Lily's wedding had sapped the fucking life out of us! Although Lily and Adam paid for most of it, Sadie, Wes, and I had left no stone unturned. We had added the bells and whistles and were beyond ecstatic to make our heartfelt contributions.

Seppie, you're going off the rails with this one. Psychology will tell you that major life transitions affect people in different ways. Lily's wedding was bittersweet without her natural parents, a mother she barely knew and an emotionally tainted father. Cut her some slack. It's healthier that she taps into and expresses her feelings through her scrapbook than to harbor them inside.

I carefully replaced the books on the shelf, balancing them across the two Mason jars. It was doubtful that Lily would know I was aware of the book but I already knew, due to my obsessive mind, that each time there would an opportunity to be alone in their apartment, I'd have an itching to check the album for additional entries. On tippy-toes, like a comic strip bandit, I had the urge to snoop around more but had no business doing so. Should I empty the jar, return it to the shelf, and bring the flowers home? My paranoia grabbed onto the best of me and I'm not even 420-friendly.

The refrigerator had a magnetic *Shopping List* pad attached to its door and I scribbled a note to leave in front of the flowers: "Welcome Home, Lily and Adam! The magic continues ..."

Neatly, I folded the shopping bags in a pile to deposit in the recycling down the hallway and collected my belongings to head home. All the while I was praying that today's discovery was simply a manifestation of Lily's struggles and the reentry into my family. Post-traumatic stress was a funny thing, you know, and could surface when we least expected it. Lily adored all of us and I couldn't fathom her not being a part of our family. She was woven into the fabric, although a different-colored thread, and I would continue to find ways to make her feel secure. She was, after all, Teddy's daughter. She was the spawn of Teddy.

CHAPTER 5

Wesley Harlow

Wes and I finally settled into much-needed alone time. With all my attention focused on Lily's wedding, the thought that I'd neglected Wes in any way made me feel sad. That man had the patience of a saint! Effortlessly, he rolled with every situation that arose by gently offering unsolicited assistance and had mastered the art of fielding the fireworks of our crazy personalities. There was no second-guessing when it came to his intentions. He asked for very little, loved to be needed, and was always emotionally available, which made him priceless!

Since I accepted his marriage proposal, he walked around calling me *wifey*, touting the fact that the next level of our relationship was official! And while I had always held a high degree of skepticism about second marriages, we fit perfectly, a relationship that had progressed naturally. It was doubtful our wedding would be an intimate ceremony if Wes and Sadie had their druthers.

Oh, and as for Elle? Our wedding would be just another event where she could wear her tiara and run her sassy mouth about whom she could marry. I'd say this much: There would be no pumpkins for her to brutalize! Buying her a blow-up doll that she could drag around as her escort might do the trick and silence her from harassing us about making her a child bride. Jesus, just thinking about that made her sound like a sleazy mail-order wife, and now I was sounding creepy!

Elle was back into her routine with Sadie and Josh. She had lived the lifestyle of royalty during the hullabaloo of Lily and Adam's wedding planning. That little spitfire, constantly entertained, had to be crawling out of her skin since the whirlwind of fun events had come to an end.

The newlyweds were delayed at the airport, according to a recent text from Lily, but I was certain that she'd reach out to us sometime tomorrow. All of us were excited to see their pictures and hear about the excursions, which had no doubt been fabulous! The two were well-suited to each other with much to look forward to as they began their voyage together. It could be a challenge to find the right match. Some believed that God was the one who put that perfect partner in our path and had little to do with one's own searching. I was not of that philosophy but did believe one could never be good enough for the wrong person but could do no wrong for the right person. Those words held truth, great merit, and had always resonated with me.

Post-Teddy, I'd ruminated how difficult it had been to made him happy, and regardless, we never would have been right for each other. Once the dark cloud lifted quite some time after our breakup, I readjusted my life and focused solely on family and outside interests that brought me pure joy.

That newfound empowerment removed the pressure of trying to reel in Mr. Right from the land of misfit toys.

Biweekly kickboxing classes remained a staple and then I added hustle lessons to my calendar. In the late 1970s, I idolized Donna Summer, aspiring to be a disco queen. I figured, what the heck? I would locate a dance studio in Manhattan and get back into dancing. Glitter Dance Studio, in Union Square, offered Wednesday-night lessons so I hopped on the Q train to dance my heart out under a disco ball. Franco, my dance instructor, fulfilled that dream as I relived my nights in Studio 54. I had a blast! As time passed, I became the most important person in my life, did not rely on hunting down a man, and finally reached the pinnacle of self-appreciation.

One evening, while returning home from Glitter, I was completely exhausted. My workday had been longer than usual, and although I had not slept well the night before, I decided to keep my scheduled dance lesson. Standing on the crowded West 14th Street uptown platform, the Q finally arrived, and the riders charged into the train car like cattle. I was grossed out at being sandwiched between people, especially men standing behind me taking the liberty to push up against my back. Was that their cell phone, murse, or something else? One never knew what was going on under their trench coats. Good Lord, such heinous thoughts! A colorful assortment of characters typically boarded and exited the train cars, and quite honestly, if someone were standing next to me with his trouser trout hanging out, I likely wouldn't notice. It was par for the course. But some big guy behind me mounting my little ladybug back like a horsefly, well, that was a different story!

Fortunately, as we approached the next stop at Herald Square a woman seated in front of me began gathering her belongings. I eyed that seat like a bear protecting her cub and got myself into the "pounce" position. Screw that! The city was an aggressive place to live, so when it came to the subways and street parking, it was survival of the fittest! Riding the subway cars was an experience, even for the streetwise. There were people who stank, those who tried to sell their shit while walking through each car, and those playing recorders or greasy harmonicas like they were performing at an indoor concert.

From time to time I'd throw in a buck or two just so these creatures could move past me. I got a rise from the ones who said they were destitute but were wearing $300 KENZOs. Those were not *Honest Abes*. For the record, I was not a heartless pig. I regularly donated to charities and causes and frequently cracked my car window to spare a five-dollar bill to those in despair walking along the FDR Drive with a sign. The subway, however, was crowded and uncomfortable so I had a tougher time with that.

Among the potpourri of straphangers, it was possible to observe some normal behavior. The man seated next to the woman ready to exit was clean-cut and engaged in reading his newspaper. My attention was drawn to him because in a crowded subway car, with few places to focus your eyes, I didn't want to be staring at some mean-ass bitch looking to gut me like a deer. When the train reached the station, the woman and several other riders exited and I slid into her unoccupied seat. Damn, that seat was golden, like sitting in first class next to an executive! My body relaxed and my eyes jutted from his hands to his face—his kind, sweet face, going home to some lucky gal.

As the train jostled me, my bumping him didn't seem to be an annoyance. I allowed the wobbles to move my body and let go of my restraint. The motion of crawling along the tracks, along with all the vibrations, lulled me to sleep. When the train came screeching into the station, luckily mine, I awoke to find my head resting on this gentleman's shoulder. He continued to read his paper and did not interrupt me.

"Gosh, I'm so sorry," I said apologetically.

He just smiled, and I could tell that he enjoyed the comfort of my head on his shoulder as much as I enjoyed the comfort of resting it there. A woman knew these things—an aura, perhaps?

The train came to a halt and both of us stood up to exit the car. I sensed he was walking behind me or it could have been wishful thinking. My trek continued on the steep escalator that climbed from the tunnel to the street level and when I turned slightly around, he was there.

"Just wanted to be sure you didn't doze off on the escalator," he said to me with a grin.

"Ah, a man after my own heart ... and safety," I replied to encourage the conversation. I missed having a connection, a feeling, even one as simple as that one encounter.

"Well, you looked very tired, and I didn't want to wake you, bring attention to your ... resting on my shoulder."

"You could have, but glad that you didn't. Thank you." I was being flirty. The escalator reached the top and he stepped off after me. Then side-by-side we continued up the short flight of stairs to the northwest side of the street. "I'm guessing we live in the same neighborhood, so would you feel comfortable if I invited you to join me now for a coffee? Java Joes is a block away and that would ensure that you'll stay awake on your walk home."

Love, love, love Java Joes! "Um, uh, yes, of course. So impromptu, but an offer I can't pass up."

"Very well, then, loop your arm through mine and let's cross the street."

He wasn't scary, intimidating, or aggressive. Just an "easy-peasy" kinda guy. I could not believe we were walking arm in arm!

We stepped into Java Joes, and he ushered me to a small table by the window. No sooner did we settle into the wicker barrel chairs than the waiter brought over two mugs of coffee with whipped cream.

"Sir, the usual?" The waiter set down the two mugs. "Let me know if there's anything else I can bring you."

"Perfecto!" he said.

"So, you're a regular here?" I laughed.

"How can you tell?"

"You must be a good patron."

I noticed that he wasn't wearing a wedding band, which I hadn't been able to see when sitting on the right of him on the train. He and I chatted away talking about the buzz of Manhattan living and discovered both of us were raised in Brooklyn. When I glanced at my watch, over an hour had passed. Strangely, I was no longer tired and must have caught a second wind.

"Wow, time does fly! Here we are as subway travel companions and coffee mates and don't even know each other's names. Mine is Seppie, by the way. But wait! Let me guess!" I raised my finger. "You look like you're a Mike or a Scott, or a ..."

"I'm Wes, and this has been a great first date."

CHAPTER 6

Subway Stories

We interrupt our regularly scheduled chapters to share a collection of subway stories from our family's finest:

The Fur Coat

On a snowy, mid-1950s winter day, in a packed subway station, my mother, then in her early twenties, squeezed into a train car to make her way into Manhattan. She planned to meet my father at his store wearing the full-length fox coat that he bought for their first-year anniversary. Money was tight, but he saved religiously to surprise her with a special gift. She could not have looked more beautiful!

All ladies, she explained, preferred to have a seat on the subway but she didn't mind standing. She placed high value on her appearance, always looking well put together. So much so that perhaps any unoccupied seat on the subway was not worthy of her ass. She found an opening toward the back of the train car with one available space on the long handrail, amongst the sea of straphangers. However, as the train barreled its way through the tunnel, she began to feel uneasy. Was she paranoid or was the man behind her breathing down her neck, too close for comfort?

His breathing became heavier, more pronounced, until almost a panting sound, but she didn't dare turn around. Finally, the conductor announced her stop and she was glad to be exiting the train. Who was this creep standing behind her? The train came to an abrupt halt; she pulled her purse in tightly to the side of her coat and grazed the back of her coat with the top of her hand, feeling a warm dampness. Terrified and embarrassed, she escaped the car swiftly, but not before turning around to get a glimpse of her perpetrator.

When my mother first shared her account of what transpired, my jaw dropped as I visualized the way this colorful event was unfolding. Okay, was my mother trying to tell me that some horndog "jizzed" on her coat? Uh, yeah, no doubt. However, she proceeded to explain that in that moment it wasn't the indecent act that had her rattled but the obscene dry-cleaning bill that my dad would have to pay. How does one retell this story to a laundry attendant?

The Transplanted Suburbanite

Jack, my easy-going, laid-back child, who had always enjoyed the serenity of suburbia, relocated to Manhattan to follow a career opportunity that he couldn't turn down. Upon graduating from veterinary school, he was introduced to a veteran veterinarian, who was close to retirement, with a lucrative practice. Jack worked alongside him for two years and then hung out his single proprietary shingle.

My son found the city to be intimidating and unsafe, from the time he was a young boy. And as he matured, the mayhem in the city streets kept him looking over his shoulder, which hampered him from enjoying the beauty of all that Manhattan had to offer. Fast-forward ... Where was his practice? Smack in the middle of Times Square! Jack's very first day traveling home from work, by subway, from Times Square 42nd Street gave him an experience that one could not possibly invent.

He recalled uneasiness walking through the streets in Times Square and passing by very few people who looked normal. Amongst the few who did were cartoon characters soliciting themselves to have young children take pictures with them; cowboys wearing a hat and boots with only a G-string, all jacked up; and whores shoving their heads in the open windows of cars asking drivers and their passengers if they were interested in paying for a nice piece of ass. Jack descended the steps to the subway station, pushed through the turnstile, then sat down on a bench while waiting for the train to approach the track.

At one point he looked up from his phone and noticed he was sitting next to a large planter sprouting dark green leaves. He rarely saw greenery in the city, but in a subway station? Impressive that the Big Apple was making strides to update the atmosphere in subway stations! Not more than five minutes passed, and the train's lights shone through the tunnel, then screeched into the station next to the platform. Jack stood up to board the train ... and so did the planter! What the actual fuck? You guessed it; it was a person dressed as a planter. I would have given any amount of money to see the expression on Jack's face as he just stood there shaking his head.

Jack snagged a seat on the train, the planter occupying

the three seats opposite him. When a young mother passed through the car with her child, he heard the boy ask, "Mommy, where is the fruit on that tree?" The creature reached his subway stop several stops later, stood up, and sauntered through the doors, "leafing" behind a few branches. Only in New York City!

Has He Lost His Head?

Sadie always had interesting stories, but the ones that were upsetting to me were those she shared years later about something she should not have been doing. And here we go …

Only recently, while we were drinking wine, her four glasses to my one, she disclosed her weed gummy story. Sadie had a night out with her girlfriends to celebrate someone's thirtieth birthday and as a gift bought a tin of cannabis gummies from a dispensary. After an evening of eating and drinking, Sadie played drug dealer and distributed one of these gems to each of her friends. What she had purchased wasn't her "usual" (as if that didn't piss me off enough) but was highly recommended based on the anticipated event.

The reaction to the gummies varied from friend to friend, and not in a positive way. Quite frankly, from what Sadie described to me in her inebriated state, I didn't know how they made it out of that establishment and to the subway. She proceeded to share that it took over an hour for one of her friends to move her legs, while another friend thought she was a hunk of meat in a deli case at a supermarket. The others were just confused. Sadie, being the least fucked up, and having mastered the art of the Gummy World and a frequent flyer at the dispensary, finally herded her friends out of the restaurant, down the street, and into the subway station. All were having a sleepover at the birthday girl's apartment.

They boarded the train; most of her troupe were not doing well, and then shortly into the ride, Sadie began having her exorcism! Things weren't looking or feeling right, and she couldn't determine if she was high as fuck or if what she was observing in the subway car was real or a hallucination. From what she described her own head space was beginning to take a wrong turn. She sat quietly to concentrate on her breathing, trying not to act like a nutcase, until she became fixated on a headless figure sitting in a row a little further down with black jeans and a bright yellow hoodless sweatshirt zipped all the way up. She became concerned that he needed assistance, seeing as how he didn't have a head! Really, now?

Alrighty, at this point I was just dead inside but inappropriately fascinated enough to continue this journey with her.

Sadie, with her motherly instincts, walked over to the decapitated subway rider and poked him on his arm. And hadn't I reinforced that she should never flirt with danger? He unzipped the top of his sweatshirt and exposed his head.

"Can I help you?" His voice sounded very normal, and his face looked like a regular dude's and kinda cute. Okay, then.

"Babe, can I get your number?"

Sadie walked away from him, returned to her seat, and tried to take inventory of what was real and what was fucked. It was beyond reproach that Sadie and The Stoner Witches found their way home.

The next morning one friend was glad that she learned how to walk again, and the other was grateful that she was removed from the deli case.

I was good. Only in New York City!

C H A P T E R 7

Wes Has a History of his Own

Now retired, it had become a luxury to focus on my children and granddaughter and especially exciting to plan European travel with Wes. He hadn't seen much of the world but had subscriptions to *Condé Nast Traveler* and *Bucket List Magazine*. Wes had married young and he and Maggie lasted less than three years. Her fear of leaving their apartment surfaced after the first few months of marriage. Her struggle to leave their home, to walk into another's, became magnified and became so incapacitating that she abandoned her job as an interior decorator.

Agoraphobia a mental and behavioral disorder, is also characterized by symptoms of anxiety. Wes recalled that the beginning signs of her disorder surfaced with obsessive thoughts about being mugged on the street. Maggie feared driving through safe but unfamiliar neighborhoods even with Wes. This, indubitably, hampered any travel for pleasure.

They honeymooned at a quaint bed and breakfast an hour from where they lived. It surprised him that he wasn't cognizant of her handicap at that point; he just chalked it up to Maggie being more of a homebody.

Ultimately, grocery shopping and other purchases were ordered online and delivered to their doorstep. Maggie requisitioned her divorced mother to stay with her when Wes was working during the day. Soon after, his mother-in-law moved into their second bedroom, the harbinger of their future. This living situation provided comfort to Maggie and a caregiver role to a very lonely middle-aged woman. Maggie refused therapy and her mother, now given purpose, supported her decision. Wes filed for divorce, which was imminent. There was no room in the bed for three people, in the literal sense.

Although never having raised children he dated women with children, but no one sparked enough interest for the relationship to accelerate to a second marriage. I can only imagine Wes' trauma from leaving a marriage where he felt powerless to take another leap of faith due to his fear of missing any red flags. I could sense that he had not experienced the fireworks of true passion, emotionally and physically, and our first few dates were handled with cautious optimism. We searched each other's eyes for trust and comfort, something both of us wanted and needed. Standing on that ledge was a tough place to be when you were offering your authentic self, wondering if that person would still be standing behind you after you'd bared your soul.

Many men whom I had met were either aggressive or obnoxiously assertive. Delivering respect and commanding self-respect were high on my ladder. People treated you by what you allowed. Several women who I know settled for a "warm body," and attaining something solid had quickly fallen to the bottom of their wish list after being on the dating circuit for only a short time. Taking chances with men I didn't know well enough, although drawn to them sexually, would leave me feeling empty if we couldn't fill the bucket together, and it was shocking how droplets trickled from their spout with little to offer. Women who resigned themselves to expecting very little got just that.

Wes and I carefully peeled back the layers, which became the real "heat." His holding back sexually drove me wild. Three and a half months into our dating he invited me to his apartment to cook dinner together. When I arrived on his doorstep, bottle of wine in hand, I had an epiphany. The feeling hit me like a ton of bricks!

Taking a chance, I remembered saying, "I feel like I am home, Wes."

He looked me square in the eye and said, "Yes, you are."

Tears filled my eyes when he spoke those words.

"Regardless of where we are, Seppie, you are home."

And just like that, just like in the movies, he tossed me over his shoulder like a rag doll and carried me off into his bedroom. For a reserved type of guy, Wes threw me off my game. I was thinking how steamy it would have been if he had cleared his kitchen counter with his forearm, dishes flying on the floor, but the "over-the-shoulder" technique, yeah, that was … yeah! I never felt surer about giving myself to a man, body and soul. The intimacy and newness of exploring another man's body could be, well, interesting and there was that hopeful anticipation that our bodies would interlock naturally, complementing good pheromones. The way in which he gave himself to me was pure and unbridled. It was all for me, all about me.

Like he had been waiting a lifetime to free himself with the right woman.

We rolled around under his sheets for what seemed like hours, his comfortable sheets, under a warm blanket with the scent of fresh linen. What we were serving up to each other was far more enticing than preparing our first dinner together. That could wait, with all the days ahead of us. And every day that followed was uncomplicated.

Sadie and Jack were the true barometers. In a short time, after being introduced, their green flags went up. Their mom had been to hell and back in a handbasket, but the truth was, I had to properly mourn the passing of my past relationship with Teddy and open myself up to the possibilities.

Discovering complete comfort in our love for each other, without other attachments, massaged our relationship into a place of accepting more permanence. Sharing my children had given Wes the experience of fatherhood by proxy. The birth of my first grandchild we experienced together, in real-time, learning about grandparenthood together. It was not to say that we didn't have disagreements, but we heard each other, not just listened. We could agree to disagree, and were never, ever, verbally combative.

Wes would likely want all the bells and whistles on our wedding day because, well, just because that was Wes! He had waited patiently to marry me and I, on the other hand, didn't need all the pandemonium. Though my nature was to be showy, I was in a good emotional space where I didn't need to draw in a crowd of friends and neighbors. I suggested that we marry on the Fourth of July with our feet in the sand, holding sparklers with our children while we watched the light shows from not-so-distant towns. A destination wedding might make perfect sense where the family could continue their own magic!

I went about the day mulling that around in my head, a destination wedding on the Fourth, but it would be one of the busiest travel weekends of the year and so might not make sense logistically. Turning our wedding into a family vacation would require coordination of schedules and taking time off from work. Ah, it was too much to think about. I decided to run it by Wes. I knew he would embrace it all, regardless of how and where we chose to recite our vows. He was an anomaly.

Wes Harlow was my needle in the haystack. Wes Harlow was what I called home. September Webb and Wesley Harlow would soon be married.

C H A P T E R 8

The Lovebirds Return to Their Nest

Ten o'clock in the morning rolled around and a call was coming in from Adam. I answered the call: "Well, good morning, Mr. Adler, and welcome to husbandhood. That was quite an affair!"

"Beyond, beyond, Seppie. First off, hats off to you for being just plain amazing, and our deepest gratitude to the rest of the family for making our celebration a one-in-a-million beautiful event. There's no end to your generosity. Lily and I were delighted to return home to food in the fridge and flowers."

"You're most welcome and it was my pleasure. Are both of you at work this morning?"

"I'm in the office but Lily took the day off. She's not feeling well and will probably call you later," Adam said, and I heard concern in his voice.

"Oh, no. What's wrong?"

"Not sure, Seppie. She was feeling under the weather the

day before we left. We dined in a restaurant off the beaten path and thought it could be a touch of food poisoning. However, I'm perfectly fine and we ate the same thing. Thank goodness her vomiting subsided the morning we left because I wasn't sure we would have been able to board the flight. Then there were delays at the airport, which added to her discomfort."

"I'm so sorry to hear that. She did shoot me a text when you guys were at the Toulon-Hyeres Airport saying there were weather delays but didn't mention anything about feeling ill. Maybe I should go over to the apartment?"

"Oh, so sweet of you, but I think she's sleeping now. It might make sense to wait until she calls you."

"No worries at all. If things change, I'm free to help."

"We know we can count on you and yes, you'll be our first phone call. Lily and I also spoke about having a small gathering at our place, family only, as a thank you, but let her tell you, okay?"

"Of course, Adam, and that's a beautiful gesture."

"Well, I have to run. Preparing for a court case so I'll leave you with a virtual hug. Do you feel it?"

"I felt it! Bye for now, Adam," I replied with a chuckle.

"Buh-bye, Sep."

That boy had a winsome personality. There was nothing not to love about him, and given Lily's past, raised by a father with a depraved mind, I prayed that she'd be able to nurture a healthy relationship with Adam. Adam's personality and demeanor resembled nothing of Teddy's and deserved to be looked upon as a clean slate. The relationship that women had with their fathers could transcend negatively or positively to their future relationships with other men. In Lily's case, there could be an underlying lack of trust or a harboring of negative opinions about men, in general. Fortunately, she had healthy exposure to my relationship with Wes and Sadie's relationship with Josh. And Jack? Well, he was nothing less than the sweetest boy on earth, and I wasn't being partial because he was my son.

At four o'clock, the *gaggle of geese* broke my concentration with Lily calling in. "Welcome back, pea," I answered after hitting the Talk button. "I spoke with Adam this morning and he told me you haven't been feeling well."

"Thank you, Seppie, glad to be back. I've been sleeping on and off, but the nausea seems to be back. I would have called you earlier," she said, her voice a monotone drone.

"Is Adam still at work?"

"Yes, he checked in with me earlier, but I told him to finish at the office. He has an important case coming up and can't afford more time off. I'll have to see what tomorrow morning brings before I call into the office to take another sick day."

"If you're not well then, you'll need to knock this thing out of your system. If it is a twenty-four-hour bug, it shouldn't last. So sorry if this put a damper on the last day of your honeymoon. I'm available to come to you tomorrow if you're staying home. Just making the offer and will stay until Adam returns. Totally up to you," I suggested.

"I will call you in the morning if I'm still not well, but I also don't want you to take a chance of getting sick."

"Lily, don't worry about me. If you're sick, then Adam can go to work with a clear head, and I can prepare dinner for the two of you before I leave. Not a problem."

"I love you for that and will take you up on your offer. How are you, Wes, and the rest of the family?"

"All is good here. Sadie took a few days off, so we had some girl time. Elle, too, of course! We're looking forward to seeing your pictures and hearing about your magical week. Just to deviate for a second, I have another thought. And please, I'm not prying. Is it possible that you're pregnant?"

"Adam and I are pretty careful, so I'd have to say it's doubt-ful."

"Just a thought."

"Interesting thought, though. Well, I need to get back into bed, but I wanted to give you a call. This is such a lousy feeling and I'm almost never sick."

"Well, if the nausea doesn't subside and you need a ride to the doctor, let me know. We'll see what tomorrow morning brings, okay?"

"Yes, Seppie, thank you. Love you."

"Love you, too, pea. Get some rest."

At eight forty-five in the evening, I noticed a missed call from Adam and immediately called back.

"Hey, Seppie, thanks for calling back."

"Of course. Is Lily feeling any better? I spoke with her sev-eral hours ago and she was headed back to bed."

"Actually, when I came home from work, I brought her to City Docs to get her checked. The nausea isn't subsiding and warm Coca-Cola, which usually settles her stomach, is not helping."

"Well, what did they say? Is it a touch of food poisoning? A virus?"

"They said that it's something that is *rattling* her system but doesn't appear to be a virus. They took a test and have their suspicions."

"Adam, what does that even mean? Is it serious?"

"Before I tell you the cause of this, the doctor said that it's likely to grow and spread. This will be an adjustment for all of us because she'll have it for life."

"Jesus, Adam, you're scaring me! I've never known Lily to be sick and this is out of the blue!" I could hear my voice trembling.

"Well, we're expecting a good outcome."

"How can I help? What is this condition?"

I heard Lily laughing in the background, sounding delirious. My screen was asking me to accept their FaceTime call. Lily looked pale and worn out and Adam was still wearing his suit.

"Seppie," Lily said, "you can help us by telling Elle she will soon have a baby cousin."

"Oh, my God, you two! I can't believe it! You're pregnant, and a good reason to feel nauseous. You scared the crap out of me! Were they able to determine how far along you are in the pregnancy?"

"No, they only gave me a pregnancy test but tomorrow morning I'll schedule an appointment and follow up with Dr. Collingswood, my gynecologist. She is highly reputable, and a woman who I work with used her as her obstetrician. I'm in good hands."

"Lily! Adam! Can I share the news with the family? I'm busting at the seams! By the way, Wes is next to me mouthing questions."

"Yes to telling Wes, but we're inviting all of you to our apartment the following Sunday for a little gathering and would like to break the news to everyone at once. Just a little get-together to say thank you for all the help with our wedding."

"You got it, no need to say more. Our lips are sealed! And I'm happy to help you set up or make something. Whatever you need," I offered with sincerity.

"That's sweet, Seppie," said Adam," but we'll likely order wraps and salads from *Agata & Valentina* and have them delivered. Sadie once mentioned to us that she caters from here, often, so it must be very good."

"Yes, she has. Pricey, but you'll be pleased. Their selection is different from the other Manhattan markets."

"I've heard that," Lily chimed in, "and Sadie always knows best, right? Only the best for her."

"Well, she certainly does her research. You'll be pleased," I responded after that little bee sting.

"We'll call everyone and hope that a late Sunday afternoon will work for everybody's schedule," Adam said.

"I'm sure it will, and all of us want to hear about the honeymoon. Listen, let me know if you need anything or want me to stop over tomorrow if you decide to stay home and take another day off from work.

"Absolutely," she said, looking very green.

I remembered having morning sickness at the beginning of my pregnancies with Sadie and Jack. With Sadie, it lasted throughout the day on some days, and with Jack, it came on strong at the very beginning of my pregnancy, then dissipated quickly. I was once told that morning sickness was a sign of a healthy pregnancy.

Wes pulled in close to me and stuck his face in the phone.

"Congrats! I will be a grandfather for the second time! We are so happy and, not to worry, our lips are zipped tight until both of you disclose the wonderful news."

"Thank you, Wes," said Lily. "We love you guys!"

"Back atcha," said Wes, holding a smile frozen on his face.

"Take care of the mommy-to-be, and we'll talk tomorrow.

Love you." I blew a kiss and then the call ended.

"Wow, pregnant," I said to Wes, feeling conflicted. "This is exciting, but they haven't had a chance to settle into married life and both of their careers are taking off. Hopefully Lily's law firm will be sensitive to the days she may have to work from home if she's under the weather."

"Who knows?" responded Wes. "Let's look at her pregnancy as a blessing. I've often heard that there are women who bolster their careers and then have difficulty becoming pregnant years down the road. I'm certainly no expert. Just what I've heard."

"Yes, I've heard that, too. And look at you! Proud grandpa bear that you are!"

"I am. I really, really am. I missed out on so much never having had children, but am very blessed for these opportunities with you, wifey."

"Oh, here we go again with the *wifey*," I laughed. "Speaking of wifey, hubby, can we talk about planning our wedding once they release the news about the pregnancy? I don't want to take away from their special time and there will be so much to do. Their apartment is tiny and I'm curious to know where they'll have room for a baby. I'd imagine, at some point, that they'll want to move to a larger space."

"Ms. September Webb. There will always be lots of things going on in our family but let's try to change that last name of yours, shall we?"

"I will be Mrs. September Harlow before we know it. It's coming down the marital river and I promise I won't stop paddling!"

C H A P T E R 9

And Then There Were Three

As expected, Lily called in to work to take another sick day and was having a rough time with the morning sickness. I picked up a box of Saltines for her to keep by her bedside and bought food to prepare for their dinner, hoping that the aroma wouldn't make her gag.

At ten o'clock I let myself into their apartment and found Lily lying on the sofa with a blanket wrapped around her.

"Hey, sweet pea," I said and walked over to kiss the top of her head. "These Saltines should help with nausea. It's not good for your stomach to remain empty. Let's try some, yes?"

"Sure. I'm glad to see you, Seppie. I called Dr. Collingswood's office this morning and have an appointment in three weeks."

"Sounds like a plan. I'll put these groceries away and if you're feeling better and can tolerate the aroma of cooking, I'll prepare dinner before I leave to go home. Just relax."

I carried the two bags of groceries into the kitchen and began unpacking. This was the first time I'd been back in the apartment since my profound discovery. Two small plates and a used coffee cup were sitting on the counter, and two cabinets were left open. I closed the cabinet where the cups and glasses were stored but needed a step stool to close that infamous cabinet above the sink. The cookbooks and creepy scrapbook were still sitting on top of the two Mason jars. That cabinet haunted me, but I was also drawn to it, curious about additional entries. Lily and I both had a sick feeling in our stomachs but for very different reasons.

"Lily, are you up to talking about the honeymoon?" I walked back to the living room and settled myself on the other end of the sofa.

"Of course, and these crackers are good."

"I'm glad. Just an old remedy."

"Our honeymoon was extraordinary! Saint-Tropez was a dream that came true. I always wanted to visit there, and oh, the trousseau that you and Sadie put together, everything French? No words."

"And the excursions?"

"We especially loved the cooking class. I'm not sure Adam and I will be rolling out croissants on a regular basis, but we had a chance to meet two very nice couples. One evening we had dinner at La Vague d'Or. It's a hotel restaurant in the Chev ... Chev ... Cheval Blanc Saint-Tropez. Their chef, Arnaud ... something with a 'D' ... Donckele, had his recipe book on display so I bought one for both you and Sadie as a small gift. I love collecting French recipe books but figured I could always borrow yours since my space here is limited."

"Anytime, Lily."

"Adam and I will have our get-together in two weeks. I'm hoping to feel a lot better by then. We'd hate to plan it sooner, then have to cancel."

"This is an exciting time for both of you, marriage and now a new bundle is on the way. Adam must be over the moon about being a daddy?"

"I suppose he is."

"Do I detect he's feeling otherwise?"

"No, I think he's happy. After we hung up with you, we called his mom. She's thrilled, being that Adam is an only child and now the family will be expanding. We only found out yesterday but talked until we fell asleep."

"And you, Lily? You'll make a wonderful mother. This pregnancy came suddenly but you and Adam seem like a solid team."

"We do, it's just that ..."

"It's just that ... what? Are you conflicted about having this baby? I'm sorry. Not looking to meddle, but I am here to listen."

"Yes, I know that. I'll need lots of support and you have stepped in as my mom. It's bittersweet that both my parents didn't live to see my wedding and now their first grandchild. If I have a girl, I'll name her Tessa, after my mother. Adam loves the idea. His dad's name was Edward so the middle name will need the letter 'E.' I'm thinking of Elle for the middle name but not sure how Sadie would feel about that. Her initials would be T.E.A for Tessa Elle Adler, and for short we would call her 'T.' Isn't that the cutest?"

"Super cute! Baby T. I love it, too. You've certainly given this quite a bit of thought. Will you find out the baby's sex ahead of time? Nowadays people are all about these reveal parties. It could be a boy."

"I've heard about those. Did Sadie have a reveal party when she was pregnant with Elle?"

"She didn't. Several years ago, it wasn't a thing."

"About the name, Adam has always liked 'Ethan,'" she continued. "I'm praying for a girl. It will be fun to dress her up like a little doll with all those designer clothes that no longer fit Elle. I'm sure Sadie would love to see them get put to good use."

"It's a compliment to Sadie and Josh that you love the name Elle. When the time is right, and you know the sex of the baby, perhaps you'll mention the name to Sadie. And who knows? Maybe during that time you may find another middle name that's unique to our family."

"Hmm ... you don't like the idea of Elle. I can tell."

"Obviously I love the name Elle, but since you mentioned it, you seem to have some sensitivity to Sadie's thoughts, and she will appreciate that. As a courtesy it's a discussion to have with Sadie."

"You're right about that. I wouldn't want to upset her," Lily responded with a long, serious stare. Her stare became an uncomfortable pause, like she was spewing out the right words for my benefit but didn't truly own them.

"But in the end," Lily smiled, "it's still our decision to use Elle."

"Of course, it is, Lily," I assured as I began picking off the polish on a two-day-old manicure.

Lily continued, "The other thought I have, which is silly, really ..."

"No, go on. Nothing at all is silly."

"Ahh ..."

"Is something else worrying you?"

"It's possible that Adam will love and dote on this baby more than on me. I want to remain the center of his world and having a baby could very well change that. Change the dynamic of our relationship."

"Lily, the love for a child is a different kind of love. To some degree, I think that new mommies and daddies carry a little bit of that insecurity, but it's natural."

"I suppose you're right. When you had Sadie and Jack did you ever feel jealous of them?"

"Sadie and Jack added dimension to our marriage. Their dad and I were married five years or so, not quite ready to have children. One morning we woke up and knew the time was right to add something to our lives that was bigger than the both of us. That's exactly how it happened. So, I guess my answer is no, I never felt jealous. I did feel incredibly special during my pregnancies and during delivery. Things will change once you're home from the hospital because there will be a different set of responsibilities. Parenthood is the most unselfish role that one can play in life because you're putting your children first. Does that make sense?"

"It does make sense. It also makes me think about how my father tortured my mother. Think about it, Seppie. Could she have sought help to find another way out? Did she really put me first when she decided to take her own life? In the end, was it better for me to grow up without a mother?"

"Pea, these are questions that we can't answer. Neither of us walked in her shoes and there may be more to your mom's story that we don't know, more than what we found in her letter to you."

"It's just so unfair that at this stage of my life, and now with a baby on the way, I have to pick through the weeds."

"There are many people who love you. Try not to think of it as picking through the weeds. You and Adam have your own beautiful garden and are growing this magnificent life together. We're all here to support both of you and enjoy life with you. And of course, there's Adam's mom."

"Did Sadie have her dad by her side when she had Elle?"

"She sure did, but this isn't about making comparisons. Everyone's life is different. Our divorce had nothing to do with our children. Our love for them is separate and strong."

I felt Lily's pain as she recited her tragedies. I didn't know another way to guide her down this path of struggle. Love and support were all that my family and I had in our arsenal. I wasn't holding a separate bag of tricks, had no magic to make this go away.

"Have you considered sharing your feelings with Adam?"

"No! Please don't do that!" Lily barked.

I was a deer in headlights and could feel my eyeballs bulging from their sockets. "The reason I'm asking is—"

"No!"

"Okay, I understand, and not to worry, but let me finish my thought. Adam lost his dad and possibly has his own feelings that he wants to explore. That may include concern for you, given your history, and uncertainty how to approach it. Or at a minimum you could verbalize that you are open to all conversation."

Having been in the mental health field, it was clear to me that Lily needed an impartial person to, as she called it, help her pick through the weeds. Marriage, and now the anticipated arrival of a baby, was beginning to unearth some deep-seated feelings. Burgeoning negative feelings that could impact this joyous time in their lives. That was beyond my purview, and Lily holding me hostage to secrecy placed me in an indefensible situation. I wouldn't dare recommend counseling, at least not today.

"I don't want you to be upset. Please, just think about it. I will hold what you tell me in strict confidence."

She threw her arms above her head and belted out, "Thank you. Wowee! I'm *sooo* much better now. I love my life, Seppie!"

And just like that, her demeanor turned on a dime.

"Yes, you do have a wonderful life," I echoed. "Are you still queasy?"

"Uh, no. I'm actually good now."

"Very well, I'm going to the kitchen to prepare roasted chicken with a side of plain baked potatoes. The baked potatoes without butter, you should be able to eat." I prepared to take my hiatus, which would separate me from our dialogue.

"Sounds good. I love you! And I love Adam, and Baby T, and everyone!" Lily sang.

"By the way," I called out from the kitchen, bringing some desperately needed comic relief to a conversation I was ill-prepared for, "you have your own bun in the oven!" Lily laughed.

Lily, like her father, was comfortable with me. Articulating her anxiety to someone whom she trusted might have been just what she needed, her cure. She was good to go, at least for now. No talk of counseling. Not today.

CHAPTER 10

Baby, Wedding, Baby

As the next few days progressed, it was incredibly difficult to keep the news about Baby T a secret. Sadie and I chatted daily, and exercising extreme caution to not spill the beans stressed me.

"Sep, I just hung up the phone with Lily and she said their trip was amazing. I didn't know you stopped over the day after they returned. Why didn't you tell me?"

"Oh, I didn't stay long. Lily had eaten something on the last day of their trip and wasn't feeling well. She called in sick to work her first day back, and the following day I brought over a few groceries."

"That was so nice of you. I'm just surprised that you didn't mention it," she stated, although it sounded more like Sadie was questioning me.

"Sorry, honey. I've also been focusing my attention on Wes. That beautiful man of mine is obsessed with me becoming his wifey."

"And rightly so, Mrs. Harlow. Should we get into wedding mode again?"

"Something simple, Sadie, with just the family. I was thinking beachy, Fourth-of-July, feet-in-the-sand kind of destination wedding. Jeez, fuck, I don't know. I'd be happy to go to the justice of the peace but I want to grace Wes with a proper celebration."

"As you should," Sadie said firmly. "Truthfully, I like a fall wedding. Late September? It's not too hot, unless it's an Indian summer, and the date would not conflict with Lily and Adam's first anniversary. What do you think?"

"I don't know if poor Wes can wait that long but I like your thinking," I agreed.

"Simple, simple, simple. Hmm. Well, what about a picnic wedding in Central Park? Yes, that's it! I heard of a company that arranges all of it. They officiate, take care of the permits, photography, flowers, everything. Unless you want a destination wedding, then ..."

"No, Sadie, keep going. You're on to something."

"I'm just thinking, all of us live in the city and organizing everything will not be as demanding."

"I like it. I'm in!" I cried. "I'm sure Wes will love the idea."

"And how cool would it be if all of us had a carriage ride in the evening? So nice, right?"

"Here we go, Sadie, always thinking out of the box. Yes, we're on the right track. I'll talk with Wes. I'm just not looking for anything over the top."

"Nothing over the top? What a joke, Sep. You're talking to me now. Nothing over the top?" she repeated, puffing.

"I'm serious. Don't mess with me, girlfriend."

"Whatever you say. Settled! Now let me begin my investigative work. It makes sense to start early. And I thought about what you might wear on your wedding day, but I'll reserve my thoughts for another day."

"Jeez, no grass grows under your feet!"

"You've got that right! Ah, Party Panache in the Park! That's it. They're the outfit that plans wedding events in Central Park. Gotta go, talk later."

Sadie abruptly ended the call and a second later the *gaggle of geese* squawked. "Hi, pea, is everything good?"

"Of course, everything is beautiful! I started back to work yesterday and I'm happy to report the morning sickness subsided. I've been making lists to prepare for T and am wondering if you'd like to go shopping with me to look at cribs. The little alcove off the living room, where we have a computer desk and some shelves, will become the baby's room. The desk we'll move into our bedroom, though it might be too cramped."

"Sounds like that could work."

"We were also thinking of buying one of those portable folding screens to serve as a partition between the living room and the alcove. There are some pretty ones, and it would keep T's room separate. Eventually Adam and I will move to a bigger apartment but for now, this will work."

"Very creative. You're on the right track, and yes, we could find time to shop for cribs."

"There's so much to prepare that it's overwhelming. I've been looking online, and the crib bedding is precious. I found one pattern that has ivory sheep against a pale pink background. I can't wait to show it to you!"

"And I can't wait to see it," I said, concerned that Lily wanted to rush into everything considering she'd found out less than a week ago that she was pregnant. She hadn't even had her first appointment with Dr. Collingsworth.

In Jewish tradition it was superstitious to bring baby furniture into the home prematurely, but I was butting out.

"Let me know if you have a few hours. It would have to be on the weekend because I'm working," said Lily.

That past week, leading up to their Sunday gathering, Lily became obsessed with the preparation for Baby T. She flooded my email inbox with websites for registries, layettes, photographers that specialized in newborns, and invitation consultants for the announcements. It remained a question whether Adam knew that Lily was possessed at this point. Maybe possessed was a harsh word to use, but it seemed suitable.

Lily had enlisted me as her partner in crime to go with her to an eleven o'clock appointment at Beau Bébé of SoHo. Frankly, I'd never heard of making an appointment to browse baby furniture, but what the hell did I know about those upscale showrooms? They planned to share their news tomorrow so I was glad that Sadie didn't ask me for my whereabouts that morning.

"T's arrival will be the buzz," boasted Lily. "Of course, it's fifty-fifty that it will be a boy and now I'm thinking, Ethan will be the first grandson. No competition there, right?"

"Not a competition, regardless, pea. Every child has his or her own special qualities. Most importantly, we want a healthy baby."

"Yes, of course. Oh, I really want to name the baby Tessa, though."

"I know you do."

Once we stepped inside Beau Bébé, a petite, attractive

young woman greeted us with bottled water and a box of animal crackers—the kind with the string handle.

"Welcome to our baby wonderland!"My name is Stephanie and I'll be assisting you." Her overzealous, high-pitched voice felt like nails on a blackboard.

Lily didn't know where to look first. Everything there was very high-end, and some cribs, quite ostentatious.

"Thank you, Stephanie." I acknowledged her as the showroom was already pulling Lily in different directions.

"Are you looking for particular pieces of baby furniture?"

"My daughter only needs a crib, as they are still in a small one bedroom. We just wanted to browse a bit. It's a bit premature to make a purchase."

"Thank you for letting me know, and not a problem. I'll leave the two of you to cruise through the rooms on your own. Ask for me if you need assistance or measurements."

"Perfect, Stephanie. We appreciate that."

"Oh, look here, Seppie!" Lily came back to get me and grabbed my wrist, pulling me over to a particular display. "Can you imagine this for T?"

A four-poster Parisian pewter crib with its canopy of delicate ivory lace stood out among the others. The crib's slim lines would easily fit in their alcove and carried a price tag of $1,950.

"Oh, and look at the duvet. How sweet! I love the lilac with its embroidered tiny silver crowns. T will have her very own tiaras from birth! I love it!"

The word "tiara" has become a sticking point with me.

Lily and I spent over an hour walking from room to room, and Stephanie took measurements and recorded some of her choices.

"Thank you, Stephanie, for working with us. Lily and I wanted to get an idea of what could work in their space, and you've been most helpful."

"My pleasure. Should you return, once you've decided, please ask for me."

"We sure will," Lily said with a smile, "and will definitely return."

The day was exhausting but I didn't have the heart to turn Lily down. Her excitement was off the chart, to the point of not being able to focus at times.

On the subway ride home, I asked Lily if Adam knew we were shopping for baby furniture today.

"Oh, no, no, no. I told him we planned to go to lunch."

"Okay."

"No need to mention it when we're all at our apartment to-morrow night."

"Whatever you wish, Lily," I replied while thinking about the wrath I'd endure from Sadie if I lied to her when asked about my day.

"Is there something that you'd like me to prepare for our get-together? I could make a dessert or bring a fruit platter," I offered.

"Oh, it's not necessary, but thanks. We are celebrating all of you for helping to plan our wedding. I'm busting to tell every-one about the baby, and the next few months will be nonstop focus on T's arrival."

"Lily, this is exciting for all of us!"

Once we reached her stop, she gave me a quick hug and exited the train.

"Love you, love you!"

"Ditto, pea!"

I continued on the train to my designated stop, relieved that our day was over and their baby announcement would come tomorrow. God help me trying to plan for their anticipated arrival and plan for my wedding. One thing I was certain of, Wes needed to become a priority now.

"How was the furniture shopping?" Wes asked when I returned home.

"Thank you for asking. Lily was beaming and she walked around as though she were in outer space. That pretty much sums it up. Kindly, just refrain from mentioning our whereabouts today. She wants that to be our little secret."

"Well, if Sadie …," he began.

"There's no mentioning it to Sadie or anyone. I have the distinct impression that Adam would not want her to be browsing baby furniture two weeks or so into the pregnancy."

"Your secret is safe with me, but I do want to set our wedding date."

"Wes, the world is your oyster. Let's propose a date. Lily is likely due around the month of May. Perhaps September will work with comfortable weather. The baby will arrive prior, and it won't conflict with their first anniversary in October. My thought was a July Fourth wedding on a beach, but Sadie thought a picnic wedding in Central Park could be beautiful and conducive to where all of us live. Thoughts?"

"Love it, Seppie! That Sadie is one creative cookie!"

"She is, and my assumption was that you would agree, so she's gathering information."

"I'm so happy right now," Wes said and kissed me before he moseyed into the other room. I could hear him singing lyrics from a Goo Goo Dolls song.

"Fortune teller said I'd be free and that's the day you came to me ...."

We were both free.

C H A P T E R 11

The Big Disclosure

Wes and I arrived at Lily and Adam's apartment shortly before 4:30 p.m. with a tropical fruit salad of papaya, mango, star fruit, and kiwi, all arranged in a teak bowl that sat nicely in a handled wicker basket. Sadie mentioned that she ordered a Parisienne bouquet from *Fleurs D'Expression*, which arrived at her place that morning. All white roses and delphinium with sprigs of eucalyptus delivered in a purple box with a twine handle.

"So happy to see you!" Lily beamed when she opened the door. "You never come empty-handed, do you? You guys are too much!"

"We're here a little early to help with any setup," announced Wes, "and you can put me to work!"

"Thank you, we are totally good."

The dining room table was pushed against the wall to make room for the seating, and Adam was arranging the chairs around the living room.

"Come on in, you beautiful people!" Adam walked over for a group hug. "This arrangement will work well since we ordered wraps and small sandwiches. We also have small bowls for the side salads. It's very informal and I hope you don't mind. If Sadie prefers, Elle can sit at the table, and we can make a place for her there."

"This is perfect," I said, "and great timing for an early dinner. Thank you for going to the trouble to entertain us. You're right, we never come empty-handed, so I put together a fruit salad. Lily, you're feeling good?"

"I'm feeling fine, just tired. My first appointment with Dr. Collingswood is next week but the office called and prescribed prenatal vitamins, which I started taking."

"As tired as she feels," Adam chimed in, "Tiger Lily here is most energized about sharing our news with the family. She adores Elle and now the focus can be on her having a baby cousin. Another little one to join the family ranks!"

"Once we are seated for coffee and dessert, I'll share the news," said Lily. "I ordered miniature cupcakes, with both pink and blue frosting, as a prelude to our announcement. Please, both of you sit and relax," she encouraged.

"What a clever idea. I love it!" I responded and could see the sparkle in Lily's eyes. All of us had traveled a long road to embrace Lily as family, and she and Adam would now be raising their own children among ours.

Wes and I settled on the sofa so as not to interfere with Lily and Adam setting up their table with the delicious creations from *Agata & Valentina*.

The sun, beginning to sink, cast its remaining sunlight over the room. It cast a shadow on the side of Wes' face, and I could no longer see the gray stubble that gave him that rugged look.

"I also have separate pink and blue paper napkins to use during dessert," called Lily from the kitchen.

"This is a special time in her life where she has a chance to shine and experience milestones with people who love and adore her," I whispered to Wes.

He took my hand in his, looked at me, and said, "And don't forget about our upcoming milestone, wifey."

"Never!" I laughed.

The bell rang downstairs, and Adam buzzed in the rest of our crew. Right on time! Their dad and I had always reinforced the importance of being prompt and considered arriving five minutes early to be "on time." We all strived to be five minutes early rather than five minutes late. They were never late!

Moments after the bell rang, there was a pounding on the door with a little voice that followed, "Let us in!"

Our princess must have run up the stairs faster than her legs could carry her. Heaven forbid she should miss one second of a party!

Wes and I stood up to greet everyone as they entered. As usual, I took the reins to settle Elle down. She often became overly excited and needed a little time to adjust when transitioning from one place to the next. It was something I'd become aware of and Sadie and I had discussed.

Adam opened the door and Elle bolted in, arms in the air. "We're here!"

Wes grabbed her and picked her up above his head, then as he gently let her down, she gave him the biggest hug around his neck.

"G-Sep, we're here!"

"Oh, we are well aware, my dear granddaughter. Now let's

help Mommy and Daddy get through the door."

"Uncle Jack is with us, too! We saw him coming down the street and waited for him."

"Well, wasn't that good timing?" I remarked.

Jack walked in with a bottle of champagne in his hand, presented it to Adam, and made his rounds to hug everyone.

"My beautiful boy, it's good to see you," I said as I nuzzled my face in his neck. I couldn't help myself. I loved him more than life and still saw him as my baby.

"How's business with your furry friends?" Wes asked.

Jack laughed. "The veterinary office is busy, and that's a good thing. My clients are always barking about something!"

"I want to go with you, Uncle Jack, to see all the puppies!" yelled Elle.

"I'm sure you do, sweetie pie. Maybe Mommy and Daddy will buy you a puppy of your own?"

"Ask them now! Ask them now!"

"Jack, you just created a monstrous situation, and I think you know that," I said with seriousness.

"Payback to Sadie for all the years she beat up on me as a kid," he chuckled.

Sadie and Josh made their way into the apartment and as I approached the door, Elle was still bumbling in the background about the fucking puppies. *Here we go again*, I thought. Pumpkins, puppies, or whatever else got into her head! I wanted to strangle my son because now we'd have to listen to that shit all night!

Sadie brought in the large purple box from *Fleur D'Expression* and Josh carried in another bag, likely Elle's bag of tricks to occupy her while the adults chatted.

"Elly, what are you yelling about back there?" questioned

Sadie with a stern look.

"Uncle Jack said you would buy me a puppy! When can we get it? I want to get one now."

"Uncle Jack said what?" Sadie saw Jack laughing. "Jack, are you friggin' kidding me right now?"

Part of me wanted to burst with laughter because this was so typical of Sadie and Jack, but trust me, the last thing you wanted to do was piss off Sadie and become entrenched in her wrath.

"Elle, calm yourself down," said Josh. "Come here and let me take your jacket off."

The men settled in the living room, with Elle and us girls gathered in the kitchen. The kitchen always seemed to be the meeting place for women.

"Sadie, what is this? This big box?" questioned Lily.

"Open it, Lily. Something special for you! Welcome back from your honeymoon. Welcome to the world of married life, and this is a token of our appreciation for hosting a get-to-gether. We appreciated organizing your wedding day."

Lily set the box down on the counter and Sadie helped her open it. Both girls pulled out the waxy paper and lifted out the flower arrangement that was securely packaged in a deep bowl filled with water and tightly sealed.

"Sadie, oh, my God! Where do you even find these things?"

"These delicate Parisienne bouquets are simply not the type of arrangement that would be sent from a florist. I special-order them and have used *Fleurs D'Expression* for several occasions. I'm really glad that you love them."

"So much, Sadie!"

"Now we need to get them out of the bowl and transfer them to a vase."

Holy fuck, a vase! I thought. *Well, that's a big déjà vu. Let's see, what about that top cabinet over the sink? The cabinet with the recipe books?*

Lily pulled over the step stool and opened the infamous cabinet. "Sadie, can you hold these books so I can grab one of the Mason jars?"

Lily handed Sadie the books, and once the Mason jar was placed on the counter, Sadie returned them to her.

She added the flower food to the jar with water and artfully arranged the flowers.

"How beautiful," I commented and carried the jar to the table.

"Let's all eat," called Adam. "Elle is ready to unwrap the food and I believe that's our signal!"

"Elly, Elly!" Sadie puffed under her breath.

Lily and Adam displayed quite a spread, and while we indulged, they described the details of their honeymoon. Elle sat on Wes' lap to eat her sandwich.

Lily walked over to the bookshelf and brought out two wrapped gifts. "Seppie and Sadie, I brought back a gift for each of you from Saint-Tropez ... with the understanding that I can borrow it. That's the caveat!" she laughed.

"You shouldn't have," said Sadie, "but I'm glad you did!"

"They're French recipe books from a well-known chef. Just another token of our appreciation."

"Where's my present, Lily?" pouted Elle.

"Elly! Daddy and I will need to have a talk with you."

Lily went back to the bookshelf and removed another small, wrapped gift.

"This is for you, Elle, for being the best 'flower-power girl' that a bride could ever ask for."

Elle tore at the paper and unwrapped a coloring book, each page with a different French food to color. Included were a set of colored pencils and a sticker book.

"Mommy, G-Sep, look! Oh, thank you, Lily!"

"Say 'Merci,' Elle. That means 'thank you' in French," said Lily.

"Merci, merci, merci, merci, merci …."

"De rien, Elle," Lily said with a smile.

Elle retired to the table where she occupied herself with her present. The adults took the chance to catch up and it felt magical, all of us together again. I wondered when Lily and Adam would begin clearing the table to make room for dessert and announce their big news. Lily must have been nervous because I was sitting on pins and needles waiting for the moment.

Sadie stood up and asked Elle to follow her into the bedroom where she and Adam placed their jackets and belongings. All of us continued with conversation, and shortly after, Sadie and Elle joined us again in the living room.

Sadie joined us on the sofa, but Elle was standing in the middle of the room with her Dora the Explorer bag. All of us waited, curious as to what she was doing. Knowing my granddaughter well, she was probably preparing for her "Show and Tell" game using her toys from home.

Elle let go of one of the handles and dug into the bag. She removed a little wrapped gift for each of us and distributed them one by one.

"Don't open it yet!" she ordered.

Everyone looked curiously at Elle except me—I was looking at Sadie.

"I'm going to count to three and then you can open your

present! Are you ready?"

"We're ready," a few of us said.

"Okay, here we go. One, two, three!"

We each pulled off the wrapping to find a baby rattle in a different color. I was confused and Lily's eyes were on me.

I exchange a puzzled look with Lily, shaking my head no to communicate that I had not shared the news of her pregnancy with Sadie.

When I turned my attention to Sadie, she was signaling Elle and nodding.

"Listen to me!" Elle announced in her acceptably cute and demanding voice, pointing her finger in the air. "Mommy and Daddy said I could tell everyone that I am getting a baby brother or sister. We don't know which one yet."

CHAPTER 12

Babies, and More Babies?

A thousand rounds of bullets rifled through me, firing emotions of elation, sadness, confusion, and devastation. Each emotion was battling for the space in my head. I was chained to that moment, commanding my reaction with no time to regroup, no time to detonate this landmine that my granddaughter had put before me in just one sentence. And just like that, a five-year-old had disrupted my universe! An ecstatic emotion filled me that would have delighted Sadie but oddly undermined Lily, in Lily's mind. Her anticipated blissful moment had just been usurped by Sadie's heavenly news. My Sadie who has the world by the balls, according to Lily.

Elle ran back to Sadie and nuzzled her face in her belly.

Jack stood up to shake Josh's hand and pulled him in for a hug.

"Congrats, bro. Love you, man! An uncle again ... I'm all in. Hey, sis ..." Jack kissed her on the top of the head. "Way to go!

Nothing like growing this family tree."

"Uncle Jack, pick me up!" demanded Elle. "Pick me up!"

Jack scooped her up and put her over his shoulder and she started flailing her arms and legs.

"Can I get a puppy instead of a baby brother or sister? Uncle Jack, you said!"

"Christ, Jack, this is all we're going to hear about for the next eight months! Elly, please! Let's not persevere on the puppies!" scolded Sadie.

"I'm not perving," whined Elle.

Everyone laughed.

"Uncle Jack will bring you to work, and you can perv on the puppies in his waiting room, okay, Elly?" Sadie suggested.

"Yay, Mommy! Yay, G-Sep! I'm going to perv on the puppies!" she yelled in delight. Jack gently lowered her to the floor and gave Sadie a *WTF? You didn't just say that?* kind of look.

"Oh, Sadie, Josh, what thrilling news!" I said with a lump in my throat. I was afraid to make eye contact with Lily.

Wes and I stood up together; he squeezed the crap out of me and said, "A grandpa again!"

"What wonderful news to share!" Adam belted out with a huge smile. "This is becoming one celebration after another! And I do mean ... one celebration after another! Let's say we have our dessert. Who would like coffee or tea?"

I'm guessing Adam was ecstatic to follow up with the news of another baby on its way to our family. Just as I turned my head to look at Lily, she abruptly stood up and exited the living room toward the bathroom. I was certain Adam didn't realize the enormity of what had just occurred. Lily sharing "their moment" with us further defined her place in our family. Her bubbly enthusiasm about her clever plan to announce their pregnancy has been hampered by Elle's grand proclamation. A bird whose wings had just been clipped and Sadie's stork was now ahead of what Lily seemed to think was a race.

As Wes and I wandered over to embrace Sadie and Josh, Elle strolled into the kitchen.

"Dessert, dessert! I want dessert! Adam said it's time for dessert. I'm ready to bring it out," she yelled.

"Honey, wait a few minutes. Come to G-Sep."

Everything was erupting all at once. My daughter and son-in-law were waiting to be smothered with joy; my granddaughter only gave a crap about getting a puppy and eating those "now controversial" cupcakes, and the apartment was synonymous with a volcano ready to spew its venom.

"Sep, it was torturous keeping this from you! We only told Elly when we left the apartment because she can't keep her mouth shut. Isn't it precious that we asked her to give out the rattles? I'm almost six weeks along so it's pretty safe to say the pregnancy's good. Oh, and we don't want to know the sex of the baby. No big reveal or any of that nonsense. There are so few times in life that we can truly be surprised."

Oh, now isn't that the fucking truth! We have a powder keg that hasn't come out of the bathroom yet, our next surprise! I pray that she can pull it all together and do the right thing.

"Where is Lily?" asked Adam.

I gave Adam a smile and he winked. Oh, he was excited to share their news.

"I saw Lily go into the bathroom."

"Look, everyone! Look what I found in the refrigerator," Elle called from the kitchen.

As Lily was coming out of the bathroom, Elle was walking

out of the kitchen with a cupcake in each hand, one blue and one pink.

"Lily made these special! Because we don't know if it's a baby sister or brother! Mommy, how did Lily know you are having a baby? Oh, look, pink and blue cupcakes! Can I eat one of each?"

The drama was unfolding and the room went quiet as the curtain was about to go up. Sadie looked confused, Lily's face was ashen, and Elle began to whimper.

"Mommy, am I in trouble?" Elle squeaked in a high-pitched voice. She turned and ran back into the kitchen. Lily followed her.

"Sep, how did you know?" questioned Sadie, and then looked at Josh. "Did you tell Sep I'm pregnant?"

"Scouts honor. Never leaked a word of it!"

"Okay, settle down," said Adam reassuringly. "There's an explanation for this."

"Why are you ruining them?" Elle cries out from the kitchen.

Sadie and I rushed in and found Lily pressing her hand down on the top of each cupcake, crushing it as the frosting oozed between her fingers.

"Josh," Sadie called, "can you take Elly out of the kitchen?"

Elle ran out to her father.

"What is going on here, Lily? Why would you do this and how did you know I was pregnant? Or did you randomly buy these cupcakes?" Sadie asked.

I was ready to interject but thought it best to let Lily speak for herself.

"It's not always about you, Sadie."

"I'm not sure what's going on here but when my Elly is crying and upset, it is about me." Sadie turned to me. "Sep?"

"This was supposed to be my night to shine," stammered Lily like a child. "The cupcakes were my creative way to tell the family that Adam and I are pregnant."

Lily's lips curled and the twisted look on her face, as she stared at Sadie, was scary. The demon lurking inside of her was setting the stage for its grand entrance, and at the expense of my daughter.

"My night, Sadie!" She poked her finger hard into her own chest, pink and blue frosting decorating her white blouse. "My night! And now everything is ruined!"

Sadie and I kept our composure, likely thinking the same thing: that Lily was not in her right mind.

"Lily," Sadie said calmly while gently brushing Lily's hair away from her eyes with her finger, "that's the best news ever! Now Elly will have a sibling and a cousin. How fun? Imagine, you and I preparing for the birth of our babies together!"

Sadie turned to me. "Right, Sep?"

"Absolutely. Our family has so many blessings that I'm losing count!"

"Lily, how about we join the others in the living room and you and Adam make the announcement? You have frosting on your blouse. Here, put on your apron and wash your hands," Sadie requested.

Lily followed her instructions robotically. She looked possessed.

And that was my Sadie, Sadie the Lady. Knowing how to handle herself, she was confident enough to put her shining moment on the back burner to come to another's rescue.

Sadie took Lily by the hand, and they entered the living room together. All were quiet. Elle's body was buried deep into Josh's as she looked down at the floor.

Lily dropped Sadie's hand.

"Elle, come to Auntie Lily. Adam and I have something special to tell you!" Lily announced with exuberance and an ear-to-ear smile. Elle pushed herself in even closer to her father.

Adam joined Lily and, after Josh gave Elle a little push, she joined them.

Lily knelt in front of Elle. "Elle, not only will you have a baby brother or sister, but you will also have a baby cousin. I'm having a baby, too!"

"More babies? Yay!" Elle jumped up and down. "But ... but, Mommy ... Mommy and Daddy ... I ... I want a puppy. Can I have a puppy instead of one of the babies?"

"No, Elly, we are not getting a puppy," scolded Sadie and then gave Jack a look that could kill.

"Elly," said Josh, "you have a very important job as a big sister and big cousin. You know that, right?"

"Oh, yes. I'm gonna dress them up like dolls! Daddy, but ... but since I can't have a puppy, can I put leashes on the babies?"

"*No!*" said Sadie and Josh in unison.

"Elle, come to your Uncle Jack. Let's try to work something out, here."

Josh and Sadie went over to hug the pregnant couple and I went over to rescue my son, who had managed to get himself into a barrel of trouble with the fucking puppies!

"I'm good," said Jack, as he picked Elle up in the air.

"Okay. Coffee, tea, and dessert coming right up!" announced Adam. "Everyone make yourselves comfortable while Lily and I bring a great end to a blessed evening!"

The evening couldn't have ended soon enough. One fiasco seemed to follow another and my brain was flooded with the emotional repair that would follow in the days ahead. No doubt, Lily was in a bad space. It could be hormonal and pushing that theory could be the escape route to massage these relationships back to normal. The trauma that Elle endured watching Lily crush the cupcakes, like an angry cartoon character in one of her favorite kid shows, had Sadie twisted, no doubt. No one fucked with Sadie or with her child. That demonic episode would have a lasting impression on Elle, indelible in her small mind. If Sadie's knickers were in a knot, which I'm sure they were, there would be a price to pay and I'd get an earful first thing in the morning.

Unbeknownst to Adam, their beautiful cupcakes, bludgeoned to death, were sitting on the kitchen counter. That should create an interesting interaction. *Thank you, but I'll stay away from door number three.*

Lily followed Adam to the kitchen, and helpful as I always am, I quietly trailed behind them. Stopping short just outside the opening to the kitchen, I heard Adam address Lily.

"What on earth happened to our dessert?"

"Oh, my God, Adam! My cupcakes! I have no clue. Let's not say anything, but I'd bet that Elle got her hands into the dessert. This is just awful! Let's get rid of them and take out the ice cream from the freezer. Please let's not make an issue of it and spoil the evening."

"Lily, I doubt very much that Elle would destroy the cupcakes."

"Trust me, that's exactly what happened. There's no other explanation. I've seen her oppositional behavior other times when you aren't with us. It's concerning that even at five years old she would behave that way. I can assure you that our child will know right from wrong."

Furtively I made my way back to Wes, harboring the damaging words that had spilled from Lily's mouth.

The evening ended on a copasetic note. Lily and Adam served two flavors of ice cream, which Elle was thrilled about. She was distracted from the "Cupcake Caper" while she decorated her mound of Rocky Road with colorful sprinkles. I tried not to make eye contact with Sadie, choking down my ice cream and shaking like a whore sitting in a church pew.

"This has been a spectacular evening! Adam and I are grateful and blessed. Sadie, you and I will enjoy our pregnancies together! Elle, you will be a big help with the babies," said Elle enthusiastically.

Talk about a 360. She's talking like nothing disturbing occurred in that kitchen.

"Aunt Lily, if I don't get a puppy, I'll bring leashes for the babies when we take them out for a walk."

Sadie elbowed Jack in his rib.

"Elly, it's past your bedtime and stop with the damn leashes," Sadie reprimanded.

"Okay." Josh said to Sadie in a soft voice, "we'll address the leashes at home." He stood up to collect Elle and their belongings.

Lily gave deep, long hugs to all of us, and her face beamed with joy! Sadie followed suit, but knowing my daughter, there was turbulence prowling around inside her.

Our family descended the stairs to the lobby, a caravan of different impressions. The men had no clue what had transpired.

Sadie and I waited on the curb for separate cabs to collect us, while the men stepped out into the street to flag them down.

"We'll talk," Sadie said.

Yes, indeed. Lily's pernicious behavior would have ramifications. There was an impending storm, and our party boat was languishing. I could feel it. Those irreparable moments were the undercurrent pulling us down, and I was afraid we were sinking.

Our taxis pulled away from the curb, away from the house of horrors, and disappeared into the night.

CHAPTER 13

Valentine's Day

"Tradition, tradition!" I shouted, snapping my fingers in the air above my head to the melody from the *Fiddler on the Roof*. "Wes, my Valentine's Day celebration is missing a small gift for the little ones. How could I have forgotten a gift for Elle, her soon-to-arrive baby brother or sister, and T? I'll run out and be quick!" I called out.

"It's freezing outside, and the streets are icy. I would feel much better if you stayed here and waited for the kids to arrive," he insisted. "Didn't you purchase gift cards? That's been your tradition."

"I know, honey. The gift cards are for the adults, but I forgot about the kiddos. Abracadabra on Lex wraps their gifts nicely and their entire children's selection is unique. Promise I won't be long. Love you, love you, muwah!" I called back, blowing him a kiss.

"You're too bullheaded, September Webb. I would take a

walk with you but then no one will be here when the kids arrive. Hurry back! And, by the way, you're not dressed warmly!"

Wes only called me by my full name when he disagreed with me and wanted to make his point.

"I will and I know. I love you, too, Wesley Harlow!"

I forcefully pulled the door closed behind me.

When I reached the lobby, I could see from the large windows that the wind was fierce. So fierce that it was aggressively whipping up yesterday's snowfall from the pavement as well as sweeping the snow off the tree branches, creating poor visibility. The snow particles viciously swirled around in the air, lost with no place to settle.

Bundled up in my not-so-warm coat, I stepped outside and quickly realized that Wes was right. It was frigid and my thinner coat would not do me justice.

"It's as cold as a witch's tit!" I said, my laughter momentarily warming me. I should have turned back to put on my thick shearling but, whatever.

Picking up the pace and walking briskly to Lexington and East 77th Street had me chilled to the bone, but their ceiling heater at the entrance gave me a warm welcome when I stepped through their doors. As fate would have it, their first display table introduced me to Elle's gift. Voilà, a magic wand that lit up! Holy fucktard, a magic wand? A magic wand! Elle was hoping for a baby sister; she and I could wave the wand over Sadie's belly and make her wish!

"Good afternoon, I'm Valentina. Is there something special that you're looking for?" a woman asked as she approached me dressed in a red leather skirt and knee-high red leather boots. The combination of her straight, jet-black hair that reached her waist, and heavy black eyeliner, reminds me of Morticia from The Addams family.

"Valentina? A beautiful name and so fitting for Valentine's Day! I think I found the perfect gift for my granddaughter, but I can use your help finding a gift for my "soon-to-be-born" second grandchild.

I picked up the wand in its purple box.

"Your name?" Valentina asked.

"I'm Seppie. Short for September."

"Very unique name, I love it," she said with a smile. "Well, Seppie, I have something in mind. Let me take the wand from you, and follow me."

Valentina ushered me to the glass counter by the cash register. "Your grandchild is due to arrive when?"

"Mid-June is the due date."

Valentina opened the glass case to remove an alexandrite stone dangling from a sterling silver bracelet. "Pearl is also considered a June birthstone, so I'll show you that, as well," she said, lifting the bracelet. "They're $95, and not sure what you are looking to spend, but I think she'll love it. Your daughter can wear this now, keeping the baby in mind, and it's the perfect Valentine's Day gift for her anticipated arrival. May I put them on your wrist?"

Valentina could not have been more accommodating and secured both bracelets on my wrist.

"Perfect, thank you! Let's go with the pearl. It's more subdued and she tends to not wear a lot of jewelry. Please wrap both of these gifts for me?" I held out my wrist for her to unclasp them, my other hand reaching for my wallet.

"Please charge me for the small gift card, too. I'd like to write a message to my granddaughter."

"Of course, and take a long-stemmed rose. A special something for our customers today." Valentina pointed to the vase.

As Valentina wrapped the gifts, I wrote a message to Elle
on the card.

"And … one more gift for a baby girl who will be born
around the same time. The mother-to-be is like a daughter to
me," I told the saleswoman.

"Very well. Do you have something in mind?"

Thinking quickly, I remembered how much Lily loved the
tiara that was passed down from generations in our family,
the one that Elle wore when she was her flower girl.

"Valentina, please tell me you have a tiara?"

"Oh, you bet I do! Follow me. This one has a clear elastic
band that goes around the head to hold it in place. It sparkles
like crazy and comes in a velvety pouch. Is $45 too expen-
sive?"

"That's fine. There is great meaning behind this gift and it's
worth every penny. Unfortunately, we don't know the sex of
the baby, but her wishful thinking is so, so strong!"

We walked back to the cash register to ring up T's gift, now
taking that fifty-fifty chance she'd have a girl.

"That will be $150.77. Here's another gift card to write your
message. No charge, it's on the house."

"Thank you. That's so kind of you, Valentina."

She placed the gifts in an Abracadabra on Lex fabric tote as
I wrote a short sentiment to Baby T.

Happy Valentine's Day, Sweet Tea,
Your present will start a tradition and Mommy will
tell you all about it!
Love G-Sep

T would be my unofficial granddaughter. It was so funny that I'd always called Lily "sweet pea," and now, I would be calling her daughter "sweet tea."

"Valentina, can you attach this card to the gift?"

"Most certainly."

I pulled a rose from the vase and added it to the bag.

"Thank you for all of your help and Happy Valentine's Day to you," I said, wrapping the scarf around my neck.

"You as well, and visit us again soon!"

The walk home seemed colder than when I left the apartment. Few people were out and about, and I fantasized that the entire world was preparing for Valentine's Day. Turning down one of my favorite side streets off the avenue, I was thinking that it would not be as blustery. But it wasn't much better with the wind whipping against my face. The street was desolate, but I loved walking past the brownstones that had their gaslights turned on. One brownstone had heart-shaped vases clustered at the top of its stoop.

Approaching the middle of the block, I saw a stocky figure sitting on a folding chair next to several trash bags waiting for weekday sanitation pickup. Strange karma. This stout figure wearing a red hat, work boots, and smoking a cigarette seemed displaced. If today weren't Sunday, he likely could have been on a service call. Well, even on a Sunday, too, I supposed, but there was no service truck. I knew this area well and something about his presence appeared atypical, a weed amongst the flowers in a Monet.

I was streetwise, a product of being raised as a city kid. Effortlessly, I carried myself with confidence, never crossed to the other side of the street in fear, and communicated well with people from all socioeconomic walks of life. Anything that sparked a negative impression was kept to myself, but my nature had always been to give every person the benefit of the doubt. We never knew the path that a person had traveled, and today could be someone's hardship. Treat everyone with the utmost kindness—that was my motto.

Red hat. Nice! Even this man is celebrating.

"Happy Valentine's Day, sir." I smiled and walked past him.

Coming up on my right were another two brownstones and I was distracted by a cluster of Valentine's Day balloons tied to the handle of one of the front doors. I could hardly wait to arrive at my front door. Surely the kids had arrived by now.

A balloon had escaped, flying high to an unknown place.

"Damn it, I should have bought balloons, too!" I grumbled.

The balloons were whipping around violently in the wind.

"Ugh," I blurted out, squinting.

Deep in thought about the balloons, a sharp pinch on the left side of my lower ribcage jolted me.

The pinch, now excruciating, came suddenly and from nowhere. A tug on my purse easily forced my hand to release it, and there was warmth traveling through my body on that very cold day. I didn't feel well.

Burn, baby burn, disco inferno. Burn, baby … I had danced to that song, "Disco Inferno," in the '70s wearing my turquoise satin halter, no bra. My body was an inferno.

The balloons were beautiful. The rest were still intact. *Please don't fly away,* I beseeched them.

It hurt to breathe, and my breathing felt labored. What was happening to me? What was happening? My body didn't belong to me.

"Oh, my g …."

I remembered the witch from *The Wizard of Oz* when she

was shrinking. Shrinking. Shrinking.

Am I the good witch from the Upper East Side? Am I shrinking?

My knees buckled and my body followed, crumbling to the hard pavement.

I'm shrinking, shrinking.

Hands out. Break your fall, girlfriend, like you tell the kids.

The street was barren.

Where are you, man with the red hat? Are you still by the trash bags, and do you see I need help? I can't get my words out.

Help me, man with the red hat. Ha, Curious George. Isn't the man with the yellow hat the one who brings Curious George the balloons?

I was winded.

Oh, Seppie, breathe. Breathe.

Where are my deep breaths? Dizzy. I'm so dizzy and nauseous. Too hard to get up but I want to go home. My family is there and where is the magic wand?

Random thoughts.

A flipbook. I made a flipbook in grade school. My life. I see it in a flipbook. Come one, come all. Come forward, you bastards. Walk the plank, malicious classmates, deceitful lovers, and backstabbing friends. Ah, I once internalized my unimportance to all of you, but you need to know that you are meaningless. Your small selves evaporated over time without ever knowing the goodness I had to offer.

I must go home so Wes can marry me. My sweet thoughts are ... I have sweet thoughts.

I was falling asleep but still a little awake.

Sadie, Sadie, classy lady. Elly, Elly, what's in the belly? Look at Baby Jack as I pull back his crocheted blanket and sing our country song. Wes, I'm coming home.

I didn't want to fall asleep here on the street with the trash.

Mama? Mama, where are you? A lamb eats oats, and does eat oats, and little lambs eat ivy. Sing that to me. And, Mamma, can you keep my babies safe?

Time to sleep. Let me sleep.

"Ma'am, can you hear me?" a man's voice calls, but it sounds very far away.

It was a deep voice, and I could hear him. Couldn't think anymore. It was way too hard to breathe. Shut off the lights.

"Can you tell me your name?" he asked calmly. "My name is Officer Beckett and I'm here with Officer Derry. We called for an ambulance."

In dreams, you had no voice. No words came out no matter how hard you tried.

"This is Officer Beckett. Squeeze my hand if you can hear me."

His voice was too far away.

Let me dream.

Up, up, and away I went in my beautiful balloon, leaving his words behind.

CHAPTER 14

The Wait

"This is not like Seppie," Wes said to the kids with a tinge of worry. "She likes to be the one to greet everyone, especially on Valentine's Day. She left the house to pick up last-minute goodies."

"Do you know where she was headed? Which store? Was she going to the grocery?" questioned Sadie.

"How long ago did she leave the apartment?" Lily chimed in.

"I tried calling her, but it went to voicemail," Wes responded.

"Let's call again. I'll try from my phone," Sadie said with panic in her voice.

"You guys arrived at 2:30 and I think she left the apartment a little after noon. Jesus, I should have gone with her, but we wanted someone to be here when you arrived. It's cold and icy out there but she can be stubborn, you know," Wes muttered.

"I can go out and track her down but have no clue where she went," offered Jack.

"Good idea," agreed Josh. "I can go with you.

"Wes, she didn't mention where she was headed?" asked Adam.

"She'll kill me for this but it's a kid's store. My brain is rattled, and I can't think of the name of it. She rushed out to pick up last-minute Valentine's Day presents for Elle and the babies."

"There's a toy store not far from here, The Toy Chest. Does that sound familiar?" asked Lily. "Or, oh, let me think, Books and Bubbles is another ..."

"Abracadabra on Lex," interrupted Sadie. That's where she shops for Elle."

"I heard my name," yelled Elle.

"Not now, Elly," said Sadie, shutting her down quickly.

"That's it! That's where she was going. And she wasn't dressed warmly enough but flew out of here."

"I'm calling the store." Sadie pulled out her phone.

"I can call," offered Lily.

"Thank you, Lily, but I'm on this."

Sadie brought the phone to her ear and cupped the other with the palm of her hand, a subtle indication that she's tuning out Lily. Her brows, pinched with concern, and eyes moving from side to side until someone picked up.

"Good afternoon, Abracadabra on Lex. This is Valentina," a smooth, but very deep voice for a woman, answered.

"Hi, Valentina. My mother's name is September and I believe she was in your store earlier? Is it possible that you'd remember her?"

"Of course, I do. And who could forget her name? How may

I help you?"

"Can you remember how long ago she left your store? She hasn't returned home yet and we're all a little worried here."

"Oh, that was some time ago. We opened at 12 o'clock and she came in shortly after that. She's lovely. Could it be that she made another stop?"

"Not sure."

"Your mom was here forty-five minutes at most."

"Well, thank you. Thank you for your help."

"Anytime, and I hope she walks in the door shortly. Bye for now and Happy Valentine's Day."

"She left the store before 1 p.m. so maybe the guys should split up and each take a different route?"

A call was coming in on Wes and Seppie's landline.

"Hello?" Wes answered, sounding winded.

"Hello, this is Officer Derry with the 19th Precinct. Do you know September Webb?"

"Yes, officer, I'm her fiancé. What happened?"

"What is your name, sir?"

"Wes, Wesley Harlow, officer."

Five sets of bulging eyes attached to ashen faces stared intently at Wes, bodies rigid. Wes waved his hand and motioned for all of us to hush. Elle was tugging on Sadie's dress and Josh picked her up.

"Can you come to Columbia Presbyterian Hospital?" requested Officer Derry in a calm and emotionless tone.

"Yes, I'll be there right away. Is she okay? What happened? All of us are worried sick!"

"We'll talk when you arrive at the hospital. Come in through the emergency entrance and I'll be waiting for you with Officer Beckett."

"Please, just tell me if she's all right, officer. Can you tell me if she's all right?"

"I cannot give you information over the phone. Just come. We're here."

The phone went silent.

"Columbia Presbyterian," Wes announced as he pressed the End button on his phone. "I need to go now."

"What did he say?" Sadie questioned, sheer terror in her voice.

"He said nothing. I know nothing. Just to meet him in Emergency."

"I feel sick to my stomach, Adam," responded Lily. "Like I can vomit."

"Mommy, why is Lily going to be sick?" Elle looked scared.

"Everything's okay, Elly, honey. Mommy has to go somewhere with Wes and Uncle Jack. Daddy will stay here with you. Adam, you should stay here with Lily. We'll call you once we get there. It's too much for everyone to go."

"Agreed," said Josh, nodding.

"I think I should be there, too," Lily intervened.

"Please, Lily. We'll call you guys once we know what happened."

Sadie saw annoyance written all over Lily's face, which was too fucking bad.

Like lightning, they bolted from the apartment and hailed a cab to the hospital. All sat silent while the cab crawled through the city streets, each traffic light bringing them closer to some tragedy.

They scrambled through the entrance in a panic, then stopped behind two people who were ahead of them at the information desk. Wes approached a security guard standing just a few feet away.

"Hello, my name is Wesley Harlow. I received a call from an Officer Derry to meet him here. My fiancé was brought into the emergency?"

One moment, please, sir. Let me check."

The gentleman unclipped his radio from his belt.

"Yes, hi. This is Devon in the lobby. I have a Mr. Harlow here for Officer Derry? He called for him to come in."

Devon nodded. "Yes, yes, no problem. I'll have him wait right here."

"Officer Derry will be right out. Just wait over to the side and he'll find you." He pointed to a corner of the lobby, away from the flurry of people.

"Appreciate it, thank you," Wes said kindly, showing composure.

"This has to be bad if the officer gave no information over the phone. They ask to see you in person when someone has died. They ..."

"Stop it, Sadie!" Jack belted out. "Don't do this!"

"I just can't. I can't ... We can't lose her."

"Please," pleaded Wes. "We need to be strong for each other. Let's hold it together and try not to think the very worst."

His words sounded well-rehearsed with no authenticity behind them, like a lawyer reassuring his defendant when he's already predicted a negative verdict. The past hour had aged him a multitude of years, the lines in his face appearing more pronounced and his body language showing defeat.

A police officer exited the doors on the far end of the lobby and approached.

"Hello, Mr. Harlow? Officer Derry. I called you earlier." He protruded his arm for a handshake.

"Yes, officer. This is Sadie and Jack, September's children."

"Please follow me," he instructed and escorted them through the large glass doors. They followed behind with an awkward gait. Sadie began to sob, and Jack held her close to him to console her.

Derry pointed to a private area.

"We'll go into this room."

There was another officer standing inside the room.

"Officer Beckett, this is Mr. Harlow and September's children."

"Thank you for coming. I know this feels scary."

"Is my mother alive? Just say it! Tell me she is going to be okay, please!"

Sadie's small frame crumbled in Jack's arms. Jack started to cry, too.

"Your mom was brutally attacked on the street," said Beckett in a controlled voice. "Someone called the precinct and Officer Derry and I responded to the call. We found your mom unconscious and an ambulance was called immediately. I'm so sorry."

"Is she … Did she … did she survive the attack?" Wes asked timidly.

"She's in the OR and the doctor will come out to see you when they know something. She lost a lot of blood. That I do know. I apologize. That's all of the information that I have. Her purse was not found with her."

"How did you know who she is with no identification?" questioned Wes.

"Apparently, she made a purchase at a store and the bag was lying on the ground. Luckily the receipt was in the bag, and we were able to track her information from her credit card number. I'd give you the bag and the contents, but we want to dust everything for prints and this is under investigation. You understand?"

"Yes, of course, officer. Thank you. Thank you for all that you're doing."

"You folks are welcome to wait in here. There's a coffee machine around the corner and as soon as the doctors know more, they will find you. Here's my card. We'll be in touch, and I'll keep you informed."

Officer Derry handed us his card as well.

"Do we need to be concerned about this person knowing our home address?" Wes asked anxiously.

"In this type of crime, the perpetrator is looking for cash. I would cancel the credit cards immediately. Typically, they remove the cash and get rid of everything else. The civilian who called the police said he didn't see the attack."

"Thank you again, officers."

"Of course, and let's think positive," said Derry.

Both officers left the room, probably relieved that their news had been delivered. In their line of work, things turned out unpleasant more often than not.

"Should we call the others with the information we have?" asked Wes.

"I'll call Josh and he can talk to Lily and Adam," Sadie offered.

"Okay."

"Wes, I don't think I can call. I'm shaking."

"I'll call Josh," said Jack.

Jack walked outside to make the call and Wes steered Sadie to the cold, cornflower-blue resin chairs that lined the wall.

The waiting was the biggest beast in the room.

CHAPTER 15

The Word

Two emotionally draining hours passed until a physician, in full scrubs, appeared at the door. His persona was intimidating and official, and he was there to deliver news that could alter our worlds forever.

"I'm sorry you folks had to wait so long. I'm Dr. Kennedy, the surgeon who operated on your mom. She was brought in in critical condition and lost a lot of blood, but she is alive."

"She's alive? She's alive. Oh, my God, she's alive." Sadie broke down.

Yes, your mother pulled through. She's in recovery but I'm suggesting that no one visit until tomorrow. She needs to heal and it's probable she won't remember the assault."

"We understand. Dr. Kennedy, can you please tell us anything about the attack based on her wounds?" questioned Wes. "We've been given no information."

"September sustained serious injuries from a deep stab

wound to her upper left abdomen."

Sadie curled up inside of Jack's arms and Wes leaned forward, arms crossed in front of him as if in pain.

As Wes pulled himself back up, he blurted out, "Oh, good God!"

"The stab wound ruptured her spleen. Splenic surgery can be tricky because we don't want to promote additional bleeding, which can affect other parts of the abdomen. We also have to be cautious of infection. We've administered a tetanus shot, obviously not having had access to her medical records."

"How long will the healing process take?" asked Jack.

"The healing can take up to twelve weeks, perhaps less. This is a lot to take in and my suggestion is to go home and get some rest. I will be calling you later to give you an update. She's in the ICU and there's a team monitoring her progress. Tomorrow, depending on how she's progressing, she may be moved to a room and allowed visitors. Whose number shall I call?"

"Sadie, Jack, if it's okay with you guys, I'll give Dr. Kennedy my number?"

"Of course, Wes," Sadie agreed, and Jack nodded.

"Very well. Let me give you a clipboard with any information that you can provide on the form for September. Insurance information and other personal information will be helpful. I suppose the officers told you that her purse was stolen so we have very little in our system," the doctor explained.

"I'm certain I can find her documents at home but we'll work on completing whatever we do know. I'll bring additional information to the hospital tomorrow."

"Perfect. One of our nurses will reach out to you later with an update. Sorry to meet all of you under these circumstances." Dr. Kennedy gave a faint smile, bowed slightly forward, and left the room.

Wes, Sadie, and Jack arrived back at the apartment early in the evening. Josh had already taken Elle back home because she was tired and irritable.

As soon as the front door opened, Lily bombarded us with a million questions.

"Lily," Adam redirected her calmly, "let everyone come inside and get settled. This has been an ordeal and I'm sure they're exhausted."

"Thank you, Adam," Sadie said, acknowledging his concern for those who just spent the most traumatizing hours in a waiting room.

"Of course," agreed Lily. "The waiting has taken its toll on all of us. I would have gone to the hospital, too. You know that."

Sadie gave her a look as if to say, *Yes, dear, of course, you would have. Piss on the tree and mark your spot.*

"Jack said that mom was attacked. Most importantly, was her surgery successful?" asked Josh.

"Yes," Sadie responded. "The surgeon spoke to us after her surgery and suggested no visitors until tomorrow. We weren't able to see her. They are carefully monitoring her in the ICU and likely will move her tomorrow. She endured a serious stab wound to her spleen. The surgeon will follow up with Wes later."

"May I ask," began Lily, "were any specifics given about the attack?"

"Let's see," chided Sadie and staring Lily down, "aside from hearing that Mom was brutally attacked and found unconscious on the street? No. We waited in agony to hear if she was still alive or if we would have to make burial arrangements."

"Lily," said Wes, "Sadie and all of us are devastated. It was a living hell hanging around the waiting room not knowing what happened to Seppie or if she survived. Let's say we get some rest and regroup tomorrow? Irritability is finally taking over, and our brains are on overload. We all love Seppie and I'm certain we'll learn more over the next few days. The police will be in touch with us."

Adam helped Lily on with her coat.

"Please keep us in the loop, even if it's a quick text. We're on call to help in any way we can," Adam said kindly. "Sadie, Lily and I could come to your place and watch Elle, in the evenings, if you want to go to the hospital."

"That would be great, and thank you both. Love you."

"I'm taking tomorrow off from work and will go with you to the hospital. It will be difficult to concentrate at work," Lily interjected.

"No problem, Lily," said Sadie. "At this point, though, we're unsure if and when we can see her. We will be taking our cues from the doctor but will certainly call you."

"Thank you, Sadie. Ready to go, Adam?"

"I am."

Sadie paused until Adam and Lily hugged her and Wes goodbye and left the apartment. Sadie could hear them padding softly to the elevator.

"Wes, will you be okay alone here? You're welcome to come back with me and stay with us for the night. You can have breakfast with Elly in the morning."

"Don't worry about me. I'll be fine here and will buzz you when I hear from the doctor. You're a sweetheart and thank you for asking. I want to gather some of your mom's medical documents to bring to the hospital."

"Fair enough. Love you, and call whatever time ..."

"You know I will. By the way, guilt consumes me. I should have gone to the store with her."

"Please, don't do this to yourself. No one could have predicted something like this in broad daylight in this neighborhood. Mom was in the wrong place at the wrong time. I don't know how I'll get that image out of my head. Only hearing about it, not witnessing it ... Well, you know how it is. Just the vision of something becomes magnified. We'll have to manage it, somehow. Lean on each other. And like the doctor said, she may not remember the attack."

Sadie leaned into Wes for a hug. When she and Jack left and closed the door behind them, strange silence hung in the air, eeriness and emptiness.

Wes sobbed.

Close to 9:30 p.m. Wes received a call from the hospital.

"Good evening, Mr. Harlow."

"Yes, hi."

"This is Nurse Kelly from ICU. How are you holding up?"

"I've had better days, thank you for asking."

"Dr. Kennedy asked me to call you. The plan to move September from ICU in the morning will depend on the kind of night she has as well as her vital signs."

He delivered the information to everyone on a group text as there was little to report since leaving the hospital. She was still alive and hanging in there, and that was a good sign.

CHAPTER 16

Pulling Through

At 10:30 the following morning Dr. Kennedy called.

"Good morning, Mr. Harlow, this is Dr. Kennedy, the surgeon who operated on September."

"Good morning, doctor, and thank you for calling. I hope this brings good news."

"Well, she pulled through the night and her recovery looks promising, but we need to keep her in ICU. She still needs close monitoring, and we want to be extra cautious."

"Has she been awake? Is it possible to see her?"

"She was awake for a short period of time but seemed confused. Normally, I would say wait another day or so, but I'm sure this has taken a toll on her family."

"It has."

"I am giving consent to have family only visit her room, for no longer than fifteen minutes."

"I understand. Her daughter and son may want to come. Is

it okay if the three of us are there?"

"Unfortunately, we allow only two visitors, one visitor at a time. For today, maybe just you and one of her children come and then we'll see what tomorrow brings. Apologies."

"No, fair enough. I'll let them know and they can decide who will be there today. Hopefully a lot will change by tomorrow."

"It's important not to question her or overwhelm her. Touching her hand is fine and reminding her of what day it is is appropriate. Even bringing a picture. No other belongings or food will be allowed in the ICU."

"Totally understand."

"Good enough. Hang in there. She's receiving the best care."

After their phone call ended, Wes got in touch with Sadie and Jack and decided Sadie would visit.

"Wes, I'm fine with you and Sadie going to the hospital today. Thank you for offering to stay back, but it's equally as important for you to be there with Mom. I'll head to work for a few hours and call me after you visit."

"We will. Let me know if you change your mind."

"I'm good. Just give her a kiss for me."

Wes sent Lily and Adam a text letting them know the circumstances for today, along with the hospital rules, and informed them that he and Sadie would go to the hospital at about noon.

At 11:45, Wes and Sadie met at the hospital and decided Wes would visit first.

Wes entered the ICU and was escorted to Seppie's room.

Beep, beep, and huff. Beep, beep, and huff.

The sigh of the machinery was loud and assuming. The

buzzing of the fluorescent lights gave the room a Halloween vibe. The room looked sterile and smelled of disinfectant.

At a snail's pace, Wes approached the bed. An IV bag hung, like a dark cloud, above her with one of many tubes invading her veins and adding to an unsettling atmosphere.

Wes pushed aside the rolling tray table and pulled the chair close to her bedside.

She looked pale and frail, and he wasn't sure he could contain himself enough to whisper any words without breaking down. Her eyes remained closed, and he covered her hand with his.

Downstairs in the waiting room, Sadie's legs shook with nervous tension as she awaited Wes' return, anxious to visit next.

A hand on her shoulder startled her, and she looked up to find Lily standing over her.

"Oh, my God, you scared me," she gasped as she placed her hand on her chest.

"Oh, sorry, Sadie, I didn't mean to do that. Adam and I received Wes' text and thought since I took the day off that I would join both of you here."

"Thank you for coming, that's so sweet of you. I'm sorry that you came all this way but only two visitors are allowed, and Jack stayed back."

"I'm sure they won't mind if I see her. It doesn't hurt to ask, I suppose."

"It's not a good idea. The doctor was very specific about no more than two visitors for a short time, and in this case it is family only. The hospital has strict rules."

"Yeah, I wonder how that would work with me. I'm family, too, no?"

"It won't work and is against the hospital's policy, Lily. As I said, Jack had to stay back."

"Wes and Seppie aren't married yet, so technically he isn't family, right?"

"Lily, are you effing kidding me? What are you trying to do here?"

"I'm trying to be a support but also want Seppie to see my presence."

"Lily, I can't do this with you."

Wes appeared in the waiting area and the timing could not have been more perfect.

"Hi, Lily, how are you?"

"I decided to join you here and didn't go in to work. How is Seppie? Is she awake?"

"She's in and out. I told her to hurry up and get better so we can get married. She gave my hand a squeeze, so I got what I needed. She looks weak. The doctor said to keep any conversation light and not overwhelm her."

"Wes, do you think we can speak to someone here about letting me see her, too?"

"I've already explained that only two visitors are permitted and it's family only," interjected Sadie, visibly out of patience.

"She's correct, Lily. Even Jack stayed back so Sadie could see her."

"Uh, I don't mean to be a pain, but I wish I was consulted." Her eyes rolled back into her head. "I'm very much like her daughter, too, and this has been torturous for me."

"Consulted?" Sadie questioned in a barely audible tone.

"What was that?" asked Lily

Sadie waved her past above her head. "I'm headed to her room. Good luck, Wes."

"She's angry with me. Do you see that attitude?"

"Lily, she's not angry," Wes assured. "Those are the hospital rules. All of us want to see her and we know how much you love her."

"And I'm *like* family as you're *like* family."

For the very first time Wes saw a flip side to Lily.

"I know you're upset and please don't be. You're welcome to wait here with me until Sadie comes back. We can discuss our observations with you so you're in the loop and can share them with Adam. We appreciate you and all your support. I hope you know that."

"I surely do," she said unconvincingly. "We'll follow up later and I completely understand. The hospital has to do its due diligence for the health and safety of their patients. I'm going to head home and hopefully I can see her tomorrow."

"It's all good, and careful going home. You're holding precious cargo!"

Lily gave a faint smile. "Thanks, Wes."

She turned to leave but not without making a stop at the information desk. After waiting patiently for the visitor in front of her to leave, she approached the receptionist.

"Excuse me, but you and the rest of your shitty hospital staff should know that your fucking rules suck! You're all a waste of my damn time!"

Wes watched the interaction from afar without hearing the dialogue and saw Lily storm out.

Upstairs, Sadie reunited with her mom and left Lily's baggage outside the door, although deeply disturbed by the continuum of her overt change in behavior. But there was a time and a place for everything, and she knew that was not the time.

Seppie slept peacefully as Sadie kissed her forehead.

"Sep, the months ahead hold the great promise of joy, planning for two babies and a wedding. It's all waiting for you."

Sadie thought to herself, *And amidst the outbreak of this impending excitement, there will be drama. Yes, there will be drama. Lily is the variable and remains the catalyst for craziness to ensue. Teddy shit on your parade, but Lily will be under our watchful eye. History will not repeat itself, my sweet, kindhearted fool.*

CHAPTER 17

The Healing

Ten weeks into my recovery and, as the doctors predicted, my body was healing nicely in the time frame expected. This ordeal was finally in my rear-view mirror. Typical me, I felt guilty that my misfortune had set everyone back. The world seemed to have stopped during the hospitalization, my mind jockeying between confusion and helplessness when sleep wasn't gracing me with brain rest. Valentine's Day and my wedding planning were left in the lurches, and then there was the added stress on my two pregnant girls.

I knew at that point that my assault had been random. Flashbacks interfered with my concentration during the most obscure times. The sight of balloons really pushed my buttons, forcing me to jog my crumpled memory to the point of nausea. Those effing balloons were doing me in!

The family had cautiously filled in the blank spaces, not wanting to further frustrate me by holding onto the information that they'd been given. Post-traumatic stress had manifested itself in one way: I had grown obsessed with my surroundings, compulsively looking over my shoulder. I supposed that was normal? That haunted street snuck into my dreams and I found myself passing by blurred figures. In that dream I was in the land of the misfit dolls with frightening faces.

I never again walked within a few blocks of the street. Times had changed.

The authorities never located my perpetrator but assured me that I wasn't a person who he or she knew; I wasn't a specific target. Likely, the offender's desperation and aggression had moved them toward the first person he or she spotted. Wes, being Wes, had become overly protective, and rightfully so. He'd become the big bear, protecting his cub in epic proportions, creating anxiety for both of us.

The Valentine's Day purchases were returned to me in their original Abracadabra on Lex shopping bag, unopened and untouched by any family member. I was pleased that everyone was respectful enough to not take a peek and allow me to decide when I wanted to distribute the gifts. I, on the other hand, would have ripped the fucker open as soon as it was handed to me.

Lily called me several times a day and had me penciled into her calendar for more "baby planning" to the extent that she became all-consuming. Her demands of me had increased, but that was to be expected, being a first-time expectant mother. She was so excited!

We were having a quick bite after her workday when I began to feel caught in the middle. Lily wanted our alone time and Sadie, if asked to join us, refused, not wanting to be pulled into our excursions. Both babies were due in May/June, roughly three weeks apart.

Both Wes and Sadie enlightened me about Lily's negative interaction at the hospital. The issue was brought up not only out of concern for me but also because we were at a crossroads regarding whether to speak privately with Adam. If Adam was observing the same behavior, we hadn't been made privy to it, but our approach, we decided, would be from a "hormones" standpoint. Adam was and had always been the most patient and agreeable man. His character was solid, and he had never said or done anything remotely questionable.

Wes leaned in close to me on our cushiony vintage loveseat, a conversation piece in our apartment and our "go to" place for snuggling.

"Wifey, don't you have to meet Lily soon?"

"I do, and I'm leaving in a few."

"I have no problem walking you there. It would be my pleasure."

"I'm good, Wes. I'm giving myself more than enough time to get there, and I'll walk slowly."

"Very well, then."

A seven-block walk would be good for me. When our lobby doors opened, I could feel that crisp air making its exit from the month of March. With springtime upon us, our individual family gardens would bloom and blossom and create an open invitation to visit.

Just a block away from Little Athena Taverna, as I passed The Book Nook, a New York Times bestseller, *Tales from the Horseman*, caught my eye in their display. A freight train ran through me. The title brought back memories of the infamous Blue Room at the Headless Horseman, where Teddy and I first met. So odd and eerie. The author, Andie Albright, was a name that I hadn't heard, and as an avid reader I was well versed on many of the best-selling authors of the age.

"Nice day for a stroll?" A woman with a nametag poked her head out of the doorway.

"It sure is," I replied, still studying the book cover showing two women outside of a blue door.

"Yes, that book is flying off the shelves. It received quite a write-up."

"I don't recognize the author's name. Is she new?"

"She is and it's an interesting read. Please, come in and take a look."

My watch showed that I had at least another twenty minutes to peruse. The restaurant was down the block.

"Have you read this book, Jo?" I asked, reading the name on her tag.

"Actually, I have, and only because it has received a ton of attention."

"Hmm, a fictional story?"

"It is. Today has been a bit slow. How about I give you 10 percent off?"

"Kind of you, yes. Yes, I'll take the book."

"Very well, come in and I'll ring you up."

I left the store with adrenaline running through my veins, both curious and excited about the read.

"There you are, Seppie," Lily called out as I approached Little Athena.

"I am here!"

"I'm glad we're having dinner because I need to talk to you."

"Let's get ourselves settled inside and you have my ear."

When we walked into the restaurant, the hostess escorted

us to a table along the wall, holding our menus, and other patrons were seated on either side of us.

"Pardon me," Lily stopped her, "can we have a more private table?"

"The only other tables are the ones in the center, but they seat four."

"That's fine, we prefer more privacy."

"Sorry, this is our busiest time, and we need to keep the tables open for parties of three or four."

"I don't want to sit there. Can I see your manager?"

"Lily, honey, that table is fine," I soothed. "I'm sure no one is interested in listening to our conversation."

"Can we go somewhere else? Now they'll lose a customer," she said in a snarky tone, her eyes on the hostess.

"Lily, please don't make—"

"Very well," the waitress said with a smile, setting down the menus on the table for four. "No problem. Enjoy your dinner. Your waiter will be right with you."

"Ah, now, that's better, isn't it?"

"Yes, but the restaurant has their system of seating, Lily."

"Whatever. She doesn't own the restaurant and the customer is always right."

A server immediately set down two glasses of water and removed two place settings.

"How are you feeling, Seppie?"

I wanted to tell her that her abysmal behavior made me sick to my stomach, but what would have been the point?

"I'm doing well, Lily. What's on your mind? There's something that's weighing on you. I would have loved for Sadie to join us ..."

"I didn't want her to join us. Wait, sorry." Her gaze dropped to her lap and then again back up at me. "That sounded bad. There are some things that I want to keep between us. There are things between you and Sadie only, right?"

I was already disappointed with the direction this was going, and once again, Sadie's name had been brought into our conversation.

"Sadie and I are both close to you and I didn't realize that her presence would not be welcomed."

"Sadie's presence is welcomed but at the right time."

I guessed she was right. There was a time and a place for everything but the way she delivered her remarks was cutting and hurtful. My blood was boiling.

"Let's take a look at the menu first, shall we?"

"Of course, Seppie."

A few minutes later our waiter approached the table and Lily and I placed our order.

"Sir," began Lily, "once our food is brought to the table, can the wait staff not interrupt us? They tend to come over way too many times. We'll call you over if there's something that we need."

"Very well, ma'am. As you wish."

The fucking nerve! They knew me as a good customer in this restaurant and my humiliation at Lily's behavior was beyond belief. Sadie, for sure, would have grabbed her purse and left.

"Seppie, there are things going on at home. I need your advice."

Dear God, please don't tell me that Adam is cheating!

"Do I need to be concerned?" I asked tentatively.

"I didn't want to say anything because all of you love Adam and ..."

"And what, Lily?"

"Well, I don't want you to think badly of him."

Here we go. She caught him cheating through a text or something.

"Uh, this is so hard."

"Just tell me. Whatever it is, we will work through it together."

"I think Adam is seeing another woman."

My body numbed.

"What?"

"If he's seeing another woman then he doesn't love me and won't love this baby."

"Lily, I'm having a hard time believing ..."

"See? I knew you would react that way. I knew it!"

"I, uh ..."

Lily looked down at her lap.

"What makes you think he's seeing another woman, and for how long—?"

"Adam never wears cologne. In the morning he is always out of bed first and leaves for work before I'm awake. He likes to get into the office very early to start his day."

"Okay, but hasn't he always done that?"

"For the past two weeks when he comes over to our bed to kiss me goodbye, he reeks of cologne. Go figure?"

"Lily, that doesn't mean that he's cheating, does it? Have you asked him about it? It's fairly simple to tell him that he smells nice and hear his response."

"No, I haven't, but I'm going to build up enough evidence to slam him with it. Just like my dad, a cheater who can't be trusted. My mother took her own life because my dad threatened to take me away from her."

"Pea, this is not the same situation and you know it. Your mom had a difficult past and Dad was angry that Mom didn't share her tragic history. Using cologne does not make Adam a cheater."

"Are you saying I'm crazy?"

"Lily, I've implied nothing of the sort. Just trying to make you see another angle. You're in your third trimester and this stress is not healthy for your marriage or this baby."

"This conversation is over."

And just like that she shut me down. Just like that, she dismissed me.

Our dinner date couldn't have ended soon enough. I signaled the waiter for the check, placed $77.07 on my credit card, and we left the restaurant.

CHAPTER 18

Tales From the Horseman, a Novel

My dinner with Lily last night generated restlessness. I tossed and turned trying to place my body in a comfortable position, but nothing induced sleep. Close to the wee hours of the morning I finally fell asleep from exhaustion but our conversation, and Lily's boorish behavior toward the wait staff, morphed into my dreams. That day, I had all to myself. I was not assigned to anyone's calendar and hopefully would not be summoned to go anywhere.

Tales From the Horseman, eyeballing me on the night-stand, commanded my attention. That would be my day to read.

Synopsis

Alice Freehold, a successful Fortune 500 piranha, finds herself swallowed up in an affair that inspires her to reexamine her choice of career over a family. The charming and wealthy Mason Muldane, a prominent financial figure, introduces her to the world of romance and alters the trajectory of her life. When Alice discovers that Mason is married with a child her fury emerges, hurling her into purgatory.

Nonetheless, Muldane's cunning and persuasive approach to keeping her tethered to their relationship seduces her on a sexual and emotional level, and her growing submissiveness emboldens Muldane to toy with her and test her limits. Is he disingenuous? Is this his game?

Muldane motivates her to think the unthinkable, encouraging Freehold to focus on the brass ring. Piece by piece they disassemble his marriage, with Alice at the helm, ending in a tragedy.

Tales From the Horseman is a brilliant work of fiction that exposes passion and jealousy, in its raw form, and the distance one will travel to achieve the perceived dream. Cleverly crafted, Albright takes her readers on a twisted, psychological roller coaster ride that never slows down.

A smooth read and quick page-turner was right up my alley! As I journeyed through the first few chapters, I found myself absorbed in every sentence with a physical discomfort. It was uncanny how Albright's description of Mason Muldane was so similar to Teddy. Were there more of him out there than I ever realized? Mason, the suave talker who met his protagonist at a business function and lured her into his cocoon. I was reminded of the movie *Up In The Air*, in which the main character, played by George Clooney, had no idea that his love interest was married.

I read on:

Our relationship solidified and Mason began sharing intricate details of his childhood, a troubled upbringing. As I pieced together his history it completed a puzzle of a boy raised by a narcissistic mother and subservient father. Both immigrants, his dad remained a wholesome man who upheld traditional family values as Mom expeditiously became Americanized in a country that offered an adult playground for everything and anything.

"My father was a beaten-down man, emotionally castrated," Mason explained to me. "My father and I feared her and I had no respect for either parent. Father cowered under her reign, no 'cojones' with which to man up. And Mom? She was a piece of work, doubling as a sex kitten with an assortment of men who visited our home when dad traveled."

"'A traveling salesman making a pittance,' she'd say. 'A joke of a man!'"

"No sooner did he leave for a business trip, our house became a revolving door for the sinners," he continued.

Poor Mason went on to say that the shrills of foreplay could be heard behind his momma's locked bedroom door. Just a child, he was still told to remain in his room for extended periods of time, once urinating on the floor for fear of leaving.

"When the giggles and moans turned to silence, that was the prelude to Momma's bedroom door opening shortly thereafter. The soft padding of footsteps down the staircase followed, then the closing of our front door, and Momma's shallow voice calling me to come out of my room."

As Mason had matured into his teenage years, his mother spun tales about his father being a financial loser.

"'I tolerate him, Mason, so you can have both parents in

the home,'" he repeated to me in his mother's tone.

I suppose that was her modus operandi to justify her infidelity. Their beautiful home doubled as a breeding ground for adultery, and without forethought, groomed Mason to be the cold and calculating man he eventually proved to be. Mom, being the breadwinner, intimidated Mason to silence, insinuating that the perils of a divorce would put his dad on the street. That was a tall order for a child to bear, so his impressionable years were filled with conflict that, no doubt, contributed to impeding his social and emotional growth.

Each chapter of his life, which he explained to me bit by bit, gripped my curiosity and left me wondering how Mason's history had manifested itself as he emerged from boyhood.

Mason and I lived two states apart, so our time together was impeccably scheduled. Extensive work travel, on my end, made our relationship a challenge so I began loosening the reins on my career to tighten the ropes on a once-in-a-lifetime chance to fulfill a blossoming romance. He became my addiction, my drug; Mason was everything. Though historically committed to my livelihood, this man was gaining speed on the inside track in the horse race of my life, quickly passing my lucrative career. It wasn't until two years later when I showed up last minute to a Manhattan work event that Mason walked in with his wife.

The devastation, well ... one could only imagine. How could he live this double life? He and I had spent our weekends equidistant from our homes to allow for maximum time together. As a savvy businesswoman I was the trusting moron, and as a shrewd businessman he was the genius. He appeared at my home in New Jersey, uninvited, with a dia-

mond promise ring.

Mason recited his wife's sordid history. It tugged at my heartstrings when I considered how Mason had been blindsided. Again, I was all in.

"Love," he said. "What we have we will never find again with another. Don't you know that at the end of this road it will be you, Mandy, and me? And if you want to adopt a child, I'd be good with that. I want you to feel that you and I share a child together in addition to Mandy."

My body tingled with joy, and waiting one more nanosecond to have the life that both of us have diligently sought after was one moment less in our journey together. Persuaded that his life with her was much less than he deserved, I decided I would be his savior.

It all made sense now. He didn't know that his wife had been a prostitute until after they married and she became pregnant. She snagged a wealthy banker and boasted about other men's desires for her, that self-serving, egotistical bitch. For the sake of their young daughter, he stayed with her, knowing that she still engaged in that vocation as his wife and Mandy's mother.

"She's nothing but a two-bit whore, no better than my mother. My plan is to leave her, Alice. Mandy is still attached to the umbilical cord so understand that it's a work in progress."

Our clock ticked away past the hour, past the days, weeks, and months as he passively worked it through in his head how to dissolve the marriage without causing trauma to his daughter. If he exposed her, then Mandy could be forever broken. During my hours alone I screamed in anger that I couldn't spend the holidays with Mason. It was maddening to imagine their cozy family sitting around the Christmas tree, and the shimmering lights that brightened their tree darkened my world.

"History cannot repeat itself, Mason. You suffered as a child, and don't you think you have a responsibility to protect Mandy? Cut the losses now?"

It had now become my personal mission to support the love of my life in every way possible. As a woman who'd been told that I could not bear children, this was my opportunity—a golden opportunity. No child should be raised by a whore, and despite never having had maternal instinct, I could be everything to Mason and Mandy. Time ebbed, and I grew intolerant of their marriage and more aggressive in my thinking, posing possible means to up the ante. Mason wanted to create "our" family, the three of us, but couldn't bring himself to pull the plug on their sham of a marriage.

"If she died, it would be less complicated," Mason joked.

I gave him an astonished look. How crass to make that comment, joking or otherwise, then his face transformed to a stare that revealed seriousness of purpose. He and I remained silent in a shroud of awkwardness.

"Let's just say, Mason, her feet should be held to the fire. She should pay for her sins in a way that will absolve you from any wrongdoing in Mandy's eyes."

"Love, I can only have a full life with you if I don't have a life with her. When Mandy is old enough to understand then that will be the right time to dissolve our marriage. You and I can continue being with each other, in this capacity."

"That will not be okay, Mason! Jesus, she's a noose around our necks."

"My hands are tied, yours aren't."

"What do you mean?"

"Whatever you'd like it to mean, Alice. You're a clever businesswoman and no doubt you've used the tricks of the trade to get ahead in your career," Mason responded in a manner that I found borderline condescending.

Mason's words were deflating, and I felt dehumanized by his description of me. I just wanted to please him, to love him and his child forever.

"Sometimes we can communicate to others," Mason continued, "that their actions are harmful, yes? I mean, my wife's behavior elbowed me to build a relationship with you and she has, more often than not, verbalized her intense jealousy. If her 'feet were held to the fire,' as you so put it, jealousy could bring a person to the brink of irrationality."

"What is it that you're trying to say?"

"Interpret it as you will, love. This dialogue is over. I don't want to discuss it again."

I never brought it up again but ruminated about our peculiar exchange. Could his wife be brought to the brink?

Dizziness and profuse sweating had overcome me. Squeezing my eyes closed I swallowed hard to dismiss the tinge of nausea creeping up in my throat. Who was this author who developed a storyline that mirrored my experience in an eerie way? How could Mason Muldane's characteristics be synonymous with those of Teddy's, clearly controlling his protagonist and exuding the qualities of the man who manipulated me? Both had a wife who was a former prostitute with a young child. The story sounded more autobiographical than fiction, yet the latter was how it had been published—as a work of fiction.

Not wanting to take a breather, and having the day to my-self, I continued to read what was quickly-emerging as Teddy's real-life story. The accounts of "Mason's" past seemed to fill in the blanks of Teddy's past. If this, unequivocally, was Andie Albright's real-life catharsis, then Teddy had shared the secrets of his childhood with her. All my gentle probing with Teddy never brought me close to this aspect of his life. It was also becoming transparent that "Mason/Teddy" had painted a very different portrait of his wife to this woman, Andie/Alice.

CHAPTER 19

Catharsis

I read for hours to quell my curiosity.

I became desperate to begin a full life with Mason and become the mother that Mandy deserved to have. Our sex was unbridled and erotic, and I turned out to be his highly skilled call girl minus the cash on the dresser. Mason was on the receiving end of inconceivable acts of lascivious behavior, something I imagined that any man would hunger for on a regular basis. Embroiled in this sick triangle and my quest to attain the dream, impatience bit me in the ass and got the better of me. Mason clearly recognized that I was relentless and now began prodding me to "find an answer" for us. His life at home became intolerable.

On a particular day I canceled morning meetings to drive to the Muldane home and parked across the street. Mason was at work, his wife didn't work, and he had no knowledge that I was lurking, waiting for his wife to exit their house.

Mrs. Muldane finally opened the front door to retrieve the mail from the freestanding mailbox at the front of their driveway. And as she did, I exited my car to approach her, careful not to trespass on their property.

"Excuse me, Mrs. Muldane?"

"Yes?"

"Do you remember me? We were introduced at The Headless Horseman during one of your husband's work events."

"I, uh, yes," she stumbled on her words.

She looked ragged and unappealing, her hair pulled up with no makeup and an out-of-style JUICY velour warm-up suit. I couldn't imagine that anyone would fuck her, although she had natural beauty. A twinge of guilt pecked at my brain, so atypical of me to ever fathom confronting another man's wife to rip her fucking world apart. I must have been possessed.

"Mason and I never stopped seeing each other. He doesn't have the guts to leave you because he doesn't want to leave Mandy. We have been building a life exclusive from whatever is going on here," I gloated as I circled my finger while pointing to their Tudor home, "and eventually you'll end up with nothing. I know your history of prostitution and, push comes to shove, Mason and I will work hard to extinguish you from the picture."

"You realize that you won't get away with this. Harassing me."

"Oh, but I will. You see, I'm not on your property and there's no record of a text or phone call. I doubt you guys have external cameras on your property and if you do, oh, well."

"You will not ever get my daughter. Mason will know that you came to our home to verbally assault me."

"I suppose it will be your word against mine, won't it? You can't prove my visit and quite frankly, he wouldn't give a shit if you did."

"You're a mistress to him. I am his wife and Mandy is our daughter. You are of no relation to him."

"Oh, but I am connected to Mason. I'm pregnant with his child and Mandy will have a sibling."

Her face became ashen, and I could see the buckets under her eyes well up with tears. She turned and walked back toward their front door, leaving the lid to the mailbox open. Her demeanor, the way she carried herself in a non-aggressive manner, was not what Mason had described. Interesting.

Several weeks passed and Mason never mentioned anything to me about my visit to their home. Unable to bear my own children, it was risky for me to tell his wife that I was pregnant with his child. If she shared that with Mason, potentially, it could have ended our relationship. My internal viciousness was seeking a place to spit its venom, and she was my target. Some nights I was kept awake thinking about how my relationship with Mason had made me fierce, a savage beast. Was that what love did to us, pushed us to succumb to cruelty in its rawest form?

On the evening of the annual event at The Headless Horseman, Mason called to tell me that his wife would not be attending. She decided to wait for him at the hotel, unable to shake a headache that undermined her Saturday routine of chores and errands. I was elated to mosey about the event with free reign to engage with Mason.

When the event ended, he and I went our separate ways, and I was pissed off that he'd be joining her. Despite our closeness, at the end of the day he belonged to another wom-an, and during these occasions I'd punch myself for taking on the role of his mistress. Plain and simple, that was all I was.

Several days passed. Mason had not returned my calls. Either she shared with him my visit to their home and he was angry, or they had rekindled their marriage. I couldn't eat or sleep and was at a loss on how to proceed. Each day I weighed myself, and the scale would drop another pound or two.

Finally, Mason reached out to me almost a week and a half later.

"Alice, my wife is dead."

My body went numb with every emotion fighting to rent space in my head.

"What? Why ...?"

"She killed herself, leaving our daughter motherless. There was no note."

And I thought to myself, This is tragic but this is our out. We are free to love each other once he finishes the cleanup in aisle ten.

"Let me come to see ..."

"No, Alice. I don't want to see you. I don't want or need you here. I want to be left alone with Mandy."

Just like that, Mason plucked me from his world like a nasty thorn in his side. Just like that, we were done.

Guilt consumed me. Once I dissected the situation, I be-lieved that he underhandedly prompted me to take action to make her go away. And now that I had, he was rid of her. I was the catalyst that made it happen. He was no more inter-

ested in me than he had been in her. My hands were dirtied with her blood, so to speak, and so were his by proxy. I gave Mason the latitude I thought he needed but he never reached out to me again.

I had nothing. I was nothing.

We had chased the rainbow in search of something magical on the other side only to find there was nothing.

And that was the true story of Teddy Zezza.

Albright had ingeniously begun her story from the end, then circled back to the beginning. Who was Andie Albright, and what was her real name? This author had created a work of fiction based upon her real-life events. *Tales From the Horseman* was her catharsis. The chapters that followed delineated her life with Teddy that led to the termination of "Tessa's" life. Little did they know that Tessa left a note.

Albright was never privy to the truth, as she, the vulture, had pecked away at a songbird's life until that bird could no longer sing. Teddy feigned information about Tessa, a woman with a heartbreaking past who struggled to survive tragedy as a young girl.

Mason/Teddy was depicted as scary. His behaviors described in the book, I had witnessed firsthand. As sexy as he was, he was equally crude, narcissistic, and diabolical. Albright reported, with clear examples, that Tessa's home life was made a misery. That translated to Lily witnessing Teddy's insolent behaviors. Where did that vicious cycle end? Teddy had no respect for his parents, became narcissistic like his mother, and Lily's personality had begun to surface as troublesome.

Albright, AKA "whomever," had respect for a man who

emotionally pummeled his wife, and conceivably, it was her last punch that ended a life. Her absolution from this love crime? Leveraging those accounts into a bestselling novel. Albright's words had freed her. Or had they?

CHAPTER 20

Eye Spy Trouble Ahead

The week was becoming tumultuous. Lily's excessive phone calls to me with obsessive urgency, obsessive thoughts, and unfounded accusations about Adam had drained me. I'm certain that our dinner at Little Athena Taverna was another turning point of her ominous and confrontational behavior, in addition to the "cupcake caper" several months ago. Wes was observant of my undue stress and that little enjoyment filled my days. Guilt consumed me, following me like a dark shadow as I battled conflict in my head. I'd invited Lily to be a part of my beautiful, intact family, and now I was lying to them by omission. Her disturbing and irrational behavior was slowly sapping the fucking life out of me.

In my plight to be everyone's everything, I didn't want to abandon the girl who had lost her mother and was ripped away from me when she was a vulnerable child. Wouldn't that have made me a monster, to kick her to the curb? Could I continue to be a big part of her life but at a distance? Did that even make sense? Sadie would have been my voice of reason, my protector, as would have Wes, but I shunned those opportunities. As I had with Teddy I lied to them by omission, but the declarations in my head remind me that more of the same never gets better. I was inviting history to repeat itself.

Not fully recovered from the attack, although healed, I had to take it easy. Lily and Sadie were preparing for their May arrivals, but so much of Lily's neediness had put a damper on my enjoyment with Sadie and Elle. Lily had become a hawk, perched high on a tree limb with her problematic, consistently inconsistent behavior, waiting to swoop down. Maybe she would have been best identified as the nocturnal owl, awake at night with heinous thoughts, watching my family sleep peacefully. I'd begun having recurring dreams about an intruder at my bedroom window. It was a moving image, neither animal nor person. And whenever it woke me, I shuffled my restless body to the window to close the blinds.

I'd become moderately avoidant in conversations with my loved ones, not wanting to be asked or answer questions.

Honk! Honk! Honk! The gaggle of geese was blowing up my phone.

"Hi, Lily, how are you this morning. Everything good?" I asked, even though I knew it was a loaded question.

"I'm at the store, not feeling very well. Not sure I can make it home."

Lily sounded awful.

"Okay, um, is there a store manager or someone who can sit you down until I get there?"

"There's a chair by the register. I'm sitting down. I'm about to make a purchase and feel my abdomen cramping up. Can you come and get me? Please?"

"Of course, I can. Have you called Adam? I can call him now while I'm on my way."

"Don't!"

"Lily, he's your husband. How can I *not* call him? Please! Where are you?"

"I'm at the Eye Spy store on the corner of Third and East 62nd."

"Lily, what in God's name are you doing there? I'll ... I'll be there. Let me speak to someone at the store."

"No, just ..."

"Not a choice. Put someone on, Lily."

"Oh, okay ..."

"Hi, ma'am, this is Vince. I'm one of the store managers."

"Hello, Vince. I'm on my way over. She's six months pregnant. Can you please stay with her until I get there? It won't take me long."

"I can. Should I call an ambulance? She is doubled over in pain."

"Just try to calm her. What happened?"

"She's been in the store for at least an hour getting information on home surveillance cameras."

Good Lord!

"I'm on my way. My number should appear on her phone. Please call me back if anything changes."

"Will do. See you in a few."

Like a bat out of hell, disheveled, there I went. A surveillance store? Really? How could I possibly call Adam? Resentfulness and anger were settling in in my struggle to uphold Lily's demands. It had reached the pinnacle and I was not serving justice here. Lily was creating a web that could not be untangled and I was smack in the center.

In my crazed and worried frame of mind, I nearly got hit by a car hailing a taxi.

"The corner of Third Avenue and East 62nd, please." I then bent my head down and momentarily rested my forehead in my hands.

As the taxi approached the store, half a block away, an ambulance with its sirens blaring was blocking the street.

"Thank you, sir, you can let me out here."

I slid my credit card through the reader, added the tip, and jumped out of the cab.

Two attendants were pulling the stretcher from the back of the ambulance, and I rushed into the store.

"Sorry, ma'am, we have an emergency here and can't let you in now."

"I'm the girl's mother. I just spoke with the manager."

They cleared the way for me to enter and, I must admit, the front of the store creeped me out. It felt like hundreds of cameras hanging from the walls and set up on table displays were inspecting me.

"Are you Lily's mom?"

"Yes. Vince?"

"Yes, I had to call for an ambulance. She started bleeding and I was afraid to wait for you to get here."

"Oh, please. You did the right thing. Where is she?"

"Come. We spread out a few of our coats and laid her down on the floor. She was doubled over in the chair."

Lily was curled up on her side. Kneeling next to her, I heard her moan softly with her eyes closed.

"I'm here, pea. The ambulance is here, too. I'll ride with you."

I could see that some blood had saturated part of her clothing. It didn't take a rocket scientist to know that was not a good sign.

The EMTs came barreling in behind me.

"Let us through, ma'am," instructed one of the technicians.

I stepped to the side. "She's around six months pregnant. Can you bring her to Lenox Hill Hospital? That's where her obstetrician is."

"Yes, of course."

I called Adam's number.

"Hey, Seppie, how are you?"

"Hi, Adam. Listen, can you meet me at Lenox Hill Hospital?"

"Oh, my God. What's happened?"

"Lily was out shopping and called me. She wasn't feeling well."

"Why the hell didn't she call me?"

And here we went ...!

Thinking quickly on my feet, I said, "Probably because she didn't want to bother you at work, and I'm home."

"Whatever. Thank you for getting there. I'll meet you over at Lenox."

"Don't worry, Adam. I'll be riding with her in the ambulance."

"The ambulance? Oh, for cryin' out loud."

The emergency team gently lifted her onto the stretcher. Her moans transcended to cries, and through her pain I heard her ask, "Why me? Why me?"

Once she was lifted up, taken out of the store, and loaded into the back of the ambulance, I jumped inside and rode next to her.

"I'm right here, Lily. Adam will meet us at the hospital, and we'll get you checked out. Just try to relax. I know you're in pain."

"Ooh, the cramps are killing me," she blurted through her sobs. "Why me? Why not someone else? Ooh, oh, this is my first baby."

Damn it, I was not going to read into that. Why her? Why not "someone" else? Meaning whom? Meaning another random pregnant woman or meaning my Sadie? Damn it, girlfriend!

The ambulance zipped through the streets, lights and sirens summoning motorists, pedestrians, and cyclists to shove off to the side of already crowded streets. In no time we were stopped in front of the emergency entrance and a crew was waiting to transport her from ambulance to intake. Once the stretcher was pulled from the ambulance, I followed her out and awaited instructions.

"Hello, I'm Dr. Forrester, one of the emergency room physicians. I'll need to take some information from you."

"Sure. Her name is Lily Adler, and her husband, Adam, will be joining me here shortly. Lily is six months pregnant, and her obstetrician is Dr. Collingswood, a physician here. She was in a store and called me because she wasn't feeling well. She has very bad cramping, and when the ambulance arrived, she was doubled over on the floor. I noticed blood coming through her clothing."

"Very well. We'll take it from here. Please just remain in the waiting area and as soon as we diagnose her condition, someone will be out to give you more details."

"Thank you, Dr. Forrester."

When the physician walked away, I contemplated calling

Sadie and Wes but decided to wait for Adam and a prognosis. There was no sense in worrying everyone.

Adam bolted in through the hospital doors and rushed toward me. He hugged me tight, then held me out at an arm's length.

"Is she going to be okay? The baby? Where are we, here?"

"I just gave them some information and they asked me to wait here with you. As soon as they make a diagnosis, they'll come and find us."

"Seppie, where was she shopping when she called you?"

Adam gave me an intense stare that impaled me like a bayonet, and I lost my proclivity for words.

CHAPTER 21

The Loss

"Lily was in a store on Third Avenue."

"Where? Was she grocery shopping when she felt sick?"

"No, she was …"

"She was … what, Seppie?"

"Adam, I …" I looked at him, my eyes begging for a "pass." He continued to stare, waiting for my reply. I looked away.

"Seppie, where was she?"

"Oh, Adam. Adam, I …"

"Seppie, I need to know where Lily was."

"She was at Eye Spy, Adam."

"Eye Spy? Is that a children's store? Like the books *I Spy*?"

"No, it's a video surveillance store."

My body felt suspended in space and Adam had a look of confusion.

"A surveillance store," he repeated robotically. "Why was she there, and did you know about this?"

"I most certainly did not, and I was as shocked as you are right now."

He sat down and lowered his head into the cups of his hands.

"Adam, Lily has been acting strangely and I'd be surprised if you didn't notice her sometimes bizarre ... Sorry, bizarre is not kind to say, but ..."

"You mean her erratic, suspicious, and accusatory behavior? I can find a myriad of adjectives to describe her behavior. The very last thing that I wanted to do was bring you and your family into the nonsense that I've been dealing with."

"Oh, Adam, I ..."

Adam composed himself and started over in a slow, deliberate, and quiet tone.

"I can only imagine, Lily being so close to you, that you carry the burden of protecting her. I get it, I really do. I've loved the crap out of that girl since we first met. Something has shifted inside her. There are threads of jealousy and mistrust, and nowadays she can't find peace in anything good that's bestowed upon her, including this baby."

"Adam, I began noticing concerning behavior at your place. The day you invited the family over to share the news of Lily's pregnancy? None of us had a clue that Sadie was pregnant. That news came as a surprise to all of us and I think it took the wind out of Lily's sails. Lily's moment was usurped by Sadie's news. There was a fiasco in the kitchen where Elle witnessed Lily destroying those cupcakes. And yes, I overheard Lily tell you that Elle must have ruined them."

"I have no words. Maybe this is her hormones, I don't fucking know anymore. In all the time Lily and I have been together, of course, we've noticed each other's idiosyncrasies, but she has become a different person. The surveillance camera makes sense because she's been accusing me of cheating on her. I now use a sensitive skin aftershave, so it automatically makes me a cheater. Lily has rummaged through our trash cans and my pants pockets, and nothing I say seems to suppress her irrational accusations."

Dr. Forrester returned to the waiting area.

"Hi, September," he said as he looked over to Adam, acknowledging his relationship with Lily. "You must be Lily's husband?"

"I am, thank you."

"Lily is with Dr. Collingsworth. Fortunately, she is on staff today and Lily does not have to see the covering obstetrician."

"Does she know anything right now? The bleeding, I'm sure, is of great concern," I interjected.

"Dr. Collingsworth will come speak with you as soon as she's made her assessment. Try to relax and remain patient. Lily is receiving the best care."

Dr. Forrester turned to leave the room.

"I pray that whatever is going on with Lily, emotionally, that she's able to care for this baby," Adam stated.

"Lily will be a wonderful mother, Adam, and I wholeheartedly agree with you. There are many women who encounter postpartum depression, who are in a healthy frame of mind during their pregnancies and it's often hormonal. It's vital that Lily approaches motherhood with the emotional availability to be positive. Even more so, to begin parenthood feeling good about marriage."

"Right now, I'm trying to get ahead of a disaster. I'm sickened by the fact that my wife felt it necessary to spend her morning looking at surveillance cameras to install in our home. That's why she didn't call me to come and get her."

I took Adam's hand in mine and cupped it with the other.

Over an hour had passed and a white-jacketed physician entered the room. I saw her looking around and then Adam and I stood up and moved toward her. Her coat had "Collingsworth" stitched in blue.

"Hi, Dr. Collingsworth, it's Adam, Lily's husband. This is her mother, September."

"Yes, hello, Adam, we have met on several occasions. September, it's a pleasure to meet you. Can we move over to one of the cubicles please, for privacy?"

Adam and I sauntered to the other end of the room, following closely behind Dr. Collingsworth.

"Please, let's sit down," she began.

Dr. Collingsworth sat in front of Adam and me.

"Adam, I'm sorry. Lily lost the baby."

I sat frozen in time, with heaviness in my chest, and waited for Adam's reaction.

"How is my wife?"

"I'd be lying to you if I told you she's doing well. Lily is distraught. The ultrasound is not picking up a heartbeat. I suspect there hasn't been movement for at least a week. I've explained that because she is almost in her third trimester that she must deliver the baby. This, for all families, is traumatic. Delivering a stillborn and wanting to see the fetus is agonizing, especially taking the pregnancy as far as she has."

"I understand," Adam said without feeling.

"Dr. Collingsworth, what caused the baby to lose the heartbeat?" I asked.

"The term is called preeclampsia. At our last visit Lily's blood pressure was very high and I had made some recommendations to her. While stress can affect the baby, it is more likely that not enough nourishment was getting to the placenta. When she was brought in today, she had already started bleeding and at this point, had lost a substantial amount of blood. I'm scheduling her for delivery."

"Will you be keeping her here?" I asked.

"Yes, they're working on scheduling her now. Both of you can see her but I must warn you, she is insisting that we stop the bleeding so she can still carry the baby a little longer."

"That doesn't make sense," Adam blurted out.

"I know it doesn't and I've seen extreme reactions from patients who can't come to terms with letting go of their baby."

"Jesus! Seppie, can you come with me?"

"Are you sure that's a good idea?"

"Please, if you want to, you can stand outside the room."

"Shall we head up?" Dr. Collingsworth looked at us and nodded.

The three of us approached the door to Lily's room and I noticed there was another patient in the room, with her bed closest to the window.

"Lily, Seppie and your husband are here. Can I send them in?"

No response.

Adam stepped into the room and, sheepishly, I followed behind him.

"Tiger Lily, honey, I am so sorry." Adam said in a low, kind voice. "This baby meant so much to us. We will get through this together and we will have another baby. I love you."

"When can you get me checked out of here? I want to go home."

"They're trying to schedule you now to deliver, Lily. I know this is tough."

"They're not taking my baby. I want to go home. Once the bleeding stops, I'll be fine."

"There's no heartbeat, Lily. Dr. Collingsworth told us that the baby hasn't been growing for at least a week. It's not healthy for you to keep the fetus inside you." Adam spoke to Lily in a calm tone.

"It's not a fetus!" Lily yelled. "For God's sake, it's our daughter. It's Tessa Elle. Our Baby T."

"Pea ..." I stepped over to the side of the bed to try to soothe her. "This is sad news to all of us. We're a family and will weather this together. We want you to be physically healthy and you can't hold onto a baby that is no longer growing in your belly, honey."

"It's unfair that *others* are having second babies when I'm trying to have one. Damn them!"

Again. A negative aspersion directed toward Sadie.

Lily tried to get out of the bed, and I could see there was blood.

The nurse stepped in front of us.

"I'm sorry, folks. We need to end the visit so we can prepare Lily. She's on the schedule to go to the delivery room in two hours, but you're welcome to wait downstairs." Then she turned to Lily. "Oh, my, young lady, where are you going?"

"I'm going home with my baby."

The nurse turned to us. "You go on ahead. Dr. Collingsworth will be along shortly. We have this."

Adam went over to kiss Lily on the forehead, but she turned her head away.

I stepped out of the room with Adam in tow.

"You can head home, Seppie. I'll wait here at the hospital

and call you once it's over."

"I can w—"

"Thank you, but I'm fine here. I need time to process everything, and you still need to take it easy. I'll be in touch with you if I need you. Just, please make calls to the family and I'll call my mom."

"We're all here for you, Adam." I gave him the tightest hug, not enviable of his road ahead, then left the hospital.

CHAPTER 22

*In Search of
Andie Albright*

The past few years had taken me down a road with unexpected curves. But springtime had finally arrived, and delightful events would soon be sprouting up in our family. The seasons ahead held the birth of another grandchild and a long-awaited wedding for Wes and me. There was so much promise for brighter tomorrows. That being said, I was concurrently being confronted with Lily's "May showers" that continued to rain on every parade.

Often, I was deep in thought about Albright's novel and her freedom from a tragic life with Teddy. Unfortunately, the saga continued for me. Lily was hitched to the back of my family's happy trailer, her deflated tires thwarting us from moving forward without negative occurrences.

I passed by the Book Nook on the way to grocery shopping and stepped in.

"Hi, how are you?"

"I'm well. Something specific I can help you with?"

"Actually, yes. Several weeks ago, I purchased the Albright novel, *Tales* ..."

"*Tales From the Horseman*," she completed my sentence. "Yes, her novel sold a gazillion copies. Flew off the shelves!"

"Well," I continued, "I read the book and found it intriguing as I'm sure most of her readers did. Is Albright her pseudo name?"

"It is. What's interesting is that this is Albright's first and only novel. I've read it too. I'm an avid reader and the creativity in her writing is brilliant. Her real name is Adriana Abbott."

"Aha," I responded.

"Albright has agreed to do a book signing here. It will be ... oh, the poster is in the window. She'll be here Thursday evening from 7 to 8:30 p.m. We will be standing room only. There's been a big response."

"I'd like to attend. Do you need to place my name on the list?"

"I'll add your name, but just to caution you, it will be wall-to-wall bodies. We have a very small space and will be at or over capacity."

"My name is September Webb, and thank you for accommodating me."

"No problem, no pro ..." She jotted my name down on her list.

"Well, then, I will see you the day after tomorrow, Jo," I said, reading her nametag and remembering her from when I purchased the book.

Thursday arrived and I told Wes that I was going to a book signing. The small photograph of Albright on the back cover of her book was not large enough to make any judgments of her one way or the other. It was small, not very descriptive, and not a professional shot. I had since googled the shit out of the name Adriana Abbott, but to my chagrin only a few items popped up, nothing that would provide me information. One Adriana Abbott I found was a dermatologist in Maryland who looked nothing like the picture, and another Adriana Abbott had a Facebook account and clearly was in her twenties. Only the title of her novel popped up in connection with her actual name.

I arrived at the Book Nook at six forty-five to ensure I'd find a seat. Most of the folding chairs were occupied and I slid into one of them at the end of a row. Looking around, I noticed that most of her audience had a copy of her book in hand, waiting for a signature. The display by the podium had several copies stacked and available for purchase at a discount.

Precisely at 7:10 Jo approached the podium.

"Welcome, my devoted customers and enthusiastic readers! Thank you for joining us this evening. By popular demand it is my distinct pleasure to introduce our in-house author, Andie Albright, to discuss her debut novel, *Tales From the Horseman*."

Sitting with nervous anticipation and picking at my cuticles, I watched intently as Andie appeared from the back room dressed business casual. She looked to be around the late fifties, with a killer body for her age, wearing a canary-yellow suit. Her high-heeled sandals with faux dandelions around the ankle straps made her look incredibly sexy with her long thin legs. I could imagine Teddy being over the moon about her.

"Welcome, and it's an honor to stand in front of my loyal readers. As a first-time novelist, an author never knows how her first book will be received but this has been a whirlwind, and I thank you!"

Andie gave a synopsis of her book for those who hadn't read it, careful not to give away too much detail. I listened intently. Questions were asked about her background and if any sections of the novel were derived from personal experience. For some, it seemed difficult to fathom that her storyline could have been contrived with that amount of passion and detail. Andie's responses all circled back to her protagonist, Alice.

"I'm so glad you asked that question," she responded to one woman. "I've taken the experiences that others have shared with me and created a very relatable character. Alice represents so many women who struggle in their love affairs with the wrong men."

Isn't that the truth? And she and I know this firsthand from our experiences with the same man, I thought.

The event was nearing forty-five minutes long and Andie closed with thanking her audience for their support and interest.

"I'm grateful to all of you for attending on a weeknight. For those who have brought your book, it will be my pleasure to sign it. If you haven't read the book and would like to purchase it, it will be only $15, a ten-dollar discount. Jo will be happy to ring up the sale. Thank you for supporting me as a first-time author."

I remained in my seat and observed the hustle and bustle of women either waiting patiently for her signature or purchasing her book at the register. Many thoughts ran through my head about how to approach Andie. During that time Lily was blowing up my phone, which I chose not to answer. After another twenty minutes passed, Andie had finished signing the books and answered a few random questions, and I stood up to approach her.

"Hello, Andie, my name is September. It's a pleasure to meet you."

"Hi, and I'm glad you came out this evening to attend! Would you like me to sign your book?"

"Thank you, but I have your book at home. Is Mason supposed to be Teddy Zezza?"

The color drained from her face. This woman who had just addressed her audience, exuding utmost confidence, became speechless. I didn't say another word but continued to observe her body language.

"Apologies if I'm making you feel uncomfortable. It's not my intent, but I read your novel and the parallels are uncanny."

No response.

I looked down at the floor to gather words for my next sentence.

"If I'm on target, this is not a work of fiction, but it doesn't matter to me one way or the other. There are a lot of commonalities in our experiences. If I am wrong about your character being Teddy, then I apologize, and I'll say goodbye. My error."

Still no response and Andie remained stoic.

"Well, then. It was a pleasure to meet you and congratulations on a beautifully written novel."

I walked over to Jo.

"Jo, thank you again for accommodating me. I'll be in again, I promise."

After I zipped up my purse I headed toward the door.

"Wait," a voice called. "Wait, September."

I turned and Andie was waving me back to the table. "Let

me pack up a few of my things and I'll walk out with you."

Bingo!

I sat back down in one of the chairs and waited patiently for Andie to gather her belongings. Once everything was packed up in her small-wheeled suitcase, she said her goodbye to Jo, and I followed her outside.

"I'm so sorry if I made you feel—"

"They say your first book is your catharsis, and this one is mine," she interrupted. "How do you know Teddy?"

"I met Teddy when he was a widower."

"I see. Teddy ended our relationship after his wife took her life. I was devastated and it sucked the life out of me. Moving forward took years. Are you still with him?"

"I am not, and Teddy passed away."

Adriana looked shocked.

"After living with him and his daughter, he threw me out. I put my life back together and have since met a wonderful man whom I'll be marrying. My daughter ran into Lily, Teddy's daughter, several years later and at that time Teddy was ill and in a facility. We embraced her. A very long story and you knew them at a different stage of his life."

"Do you want to grab a coffee? I'm only going back to my hotel but if you have time we can sit somewhere."

"Yes, surely. There is a small diner a block from here, if you don't mind a diner. We can sit in a booth."

Andie and I spent upwards of almost two hours in conversation, and during that time I texted Wes to tell him that I ran into a friend whom I hadn't seen.

"My real name is Adriana, by the way."

"Well, it's a pleasure, Adriana."

Adriana filled in the spaces of Teddy's earlier years, and I brought her up to speed with the years that I had been with him. I shared Lily's connection to my family, as well as the letter that was found taped to the back of their house safe by Tessa.

"I don't even know what to say," Adriana said, confused. "He outwardly lied about his wife's prostitution during their marriage."

"And he lied to me about her terminal illness. I hear and feel your pain and relate to every word that's written in your book. What I didn't have is insight into his childhood. It appears that you and I took circuitous routes to try to get to a positive destination after our relationship with him. Turning up empty is something I can identify with firsthand. I hear and feel that devastation."

Time flew and our meeting each other was liberating on many levels, for both of us. She had since forged ahead and married a corporate hotshot, which sounded more like a marriage of convenience, but, hey, who was I to judge?

"Adriana, it's getting late, and I need to head back. Thank you. Thank you for your honesty, and sharing, and I wish the best for both of us."

"Oh, and I the same for you. Would you like to exchange numbers and stay in touch? I live in the Boston area but frequently fly to New York."

"This has been good and brings closure to the many questions that loomed over both of us for years. I'm in a comfortable place in my life, as I believe you are from our conversation. Please don't take this in the wrong vein but for my own self-preservation, the Teddy Zezza chapter has to remain closed. It's a toxicity that has taken years to shed. I hope you understand."

"I really do, but should you ever want to reach out I am leaving you my card." She pulled one from her case. "I'm taking care of the bill."

We stood up and hugged.

"Be well. I mean that sincerely," I said.

And I turned to leave without looking back. She and I had a lot to digest without having anything more than a coffee, but I had found another dimension of peace.

CHAPTER 23

A Baby Sprinkle

Lily delivered her stillborn baby girl. Sadie's baby was alive and kicking in her belly.

Though she had already had a major personality shift prior to this unfortunate event, Lily hence became more embittered, exhibiting bizarre behavior to complement that fact. After healing from the delivery, she returned to work in maternity clothes with padding underneath to appear "still pregnant." Adam noticed several additional online purchases for "Baby T" on their joint credit card, ordered after Lily was released from the hospital, and his continued encouragement for couples counseling has reached a dead end.

Sadie had overextended herself in every way possible, but for obvious reasons, Lily had difficulty connecting with her. Life, as we knew it, had been turned upside down. Adam spent little time at home and propelled himself into additional work hours because their marriage was strained.

I was planning a baby sprinkle for my Sadie, and meanwhile, Sadie was planning my wedding. I wanted to indulge in the preparation of my second grandchild's arrival, free of heart and expression. I knew involving Lily would likely stoke her ferocious fire, but I still wanted to include her. Wes encouraged me to make the offer and let Lily decide. He did have a point that it should be Lily's decision.

"Hi, pea, it's Sep. How are you doing today?"

"Great, Seppie, really good."

"So glad to hear. Listen, and please be honest with me, okay?"

"Of course. What is it?"

"I want to plan a baby sprinkle for Sadie and would love for you to help me. Please, I completely understand if it's too—"

"Really? Of course, I'd want to plan that with you. Sadie is my sister, after all."

"Well, oh ... okay! I'm looking forward to your ideas."

"Sep, I already have some thoughts brewing. Do you want to come over and I'll make us a lunch?"

"Uh, yes. So, you've given this some thought, have you?"

"I have. Let's do it Sunday, maybe 11:30ish?"

"Can we do it a little earlier? Only because I have plans with Sadie and Elle at one o'clock and I don't want to rush you."

"Sadie and Elle, yes. Yes, of course. Sadie and Elle."

I heard the sharpness in her tone.

"Fine, come over at eleven and I'll have you out in time for your Girls' Day."

Ouch!

"We're just going to head over to—"

"It's fine, Seppie. Eleven is fine."

Lily ended the call.

Sunday rolled around, and I ended up on Lily's doorstep precisely at eleven o'clock.

"Welcome, Sep. I made us a fabulous little brunch. I hope you're hungry."

"Indeed I am."

The table was set with salads and bagels, and I could smell the coffee brewing from the kitchen.

I've thought about what both Sadie and Lily's baby showers would have looked like had Lily not lost her baby. Due around the same time, perhaps we could have planned a double celebration. However, knowing Lily, she would have wanted her own and would have seen a joint shower as an infringement on her special moment.

While Lily continued to gather a few last-minute items from the kitchen, I took a peek around. Baby T's room was set up in full bloom, waiting, sadly, for no anticipated arrival. Inside the crib was the padding that Lily used underneath her clothing. I wanted to cry.

"Okay, let's eat and discuss the party, Sep."

I strolled back to the table. "I'm glad we have some alone time, Lily. How are you and Adam doing?" I knew full well that Adam was struggling in the marriage.

"Oh, I don't know. Just the same, I guess. He's the same lying sack of shit as always. I told him that I'll continue to walk around looking pregnant until he gets me pregnant again."

"And he doesn't want to try for another baby?" I asked, cross-eyed, normalizing a conversation that had no soft place to land. Lily was like a kangaroo hopping around with a stuffed joey in its marsupium!

"It's his fault our Baby T died. He put all this stress on me by making me mistrust him. It's his fault, you know. And I don't want to discuss it if you don't mind."

"No, I don't mind. I'm only checking in with you."

"So, this baby sprinkle ... Let's put our thoughts together, shall we?" Lily announced with a great big smile, her pendulum swinging from the negative to the positive.

"Well, we'll be having it at Suzie's Wild West in the Upper West. Its interior is a saloon with farm-to-table food, and there is a mechanical bull in the center of the room. Sadie's been there with Josh and their friends, and she's always loved anything with a western theme. Private seating upstairs seats thirty people max. The guys can join us afterward."

"Western? Doesn't seem the right style for a baby shower, Sep, but I can work with that. Have you booked it?"

"Yes, I left a deposit. Sadie is due the second week in June so I was thinking the last Sunday in May, Memorial weekend? The maître d' said the city is a ghost town on that weekend, with everyone escaping to the Hamptons and wherever. A Sunday afternoon from 3 to 6 p.m. won't put a damper on any friends who will be away. Josh will get her and Elle there and will tell her that he made a reservation."

"Sounds good," she responded in an unenthusiastic, accommodating tone. "Since we don't know the sex of the baby, and Sadie doesn't want a 'reveal,' let's do baby-pink and powder-blue cowboy hats. I've seen them online. What do you think? We can also buy bandanas in pink and blue."

"I love that idea! I knew you would come up with something fantastic and creative."

She and I enjoyed lunch and rifled through a few online catalogs.

"Sep, leave it to me. I'm really good at this!"

"Well, okay then, it sounds like a good plan, and I'll reimburse you for the cost of what you lay out. This puts me over-the-moon happy that we're making Sadie's shower together."

Lily tapped her phone screen to check the time.

"You'd better scoot out," Lily said with an awkward stare, the sides of her mouth turned up into a twisted smile. "It's almost that witching hour." Her voice sounding deep and creepy, her eyes opening wide while she fluttered her fingers. "We don't want Sadie to turn into a pumpkin if you're not on time to meet her and precious little Elle."

And there was the dig!

"Lily, I can't get a read on why you would make a comment like that," I remarked, knowing full well it was jealousy.

"Oh, c'mon, I'm joking. You know how much I adore those two."

Her response left me with no defense, and somehow, I still managed to find ways to trust her good intentions.

"Let me bring some dishes into the kitchen before I go."

"Not necessary. I'm home alone all day. Once I clean up, I'll have time to start working on the shower while you girls are out gallivanting."

Dig number two.

Lily's personality reared its ugly head in ways that I had experienced with her father. There was sweetness, yes, but it was bittersweet. For her every good deed and thought there were caveats, a cutting remark, and a hint of jealousy. Jealousy was the root of evil. Her family tree had fragmented at its core with paternal deceit, emotional abuse, and infidelity, which shattered a child's self-worth and trust. I had endured tremendous guilt for loving her so much when she was a young child, carrying her under my wing when Teddy died and flying her to the highest branch of my family tree to safety.

I gathered my things.

"Give me a tight hug, sweet pea, and know how much I appreciate that we're planning this party together."

"I won't disappoint you. I'm totally good."

Sadness overpowered my other emotions as I left the apartment, sadness about Lily. Lily, alone with the dirty dishes, her dirty thoughts of my Sadie, dirty lies about her husband, and the maternity pillow form that she had pilfered off a mannequin, occupying a clean crib that waited for no baby.

The weeks that followed were odd. Lily followed through on her purchases for Sadie's shower. I'd stopped over at her apartment and saw boxes of decorations, including the adorable felt cowboy hats. I'd sent out the invitations through snail mail, as I detested evites, although that would have been easier to manage. Call me old-fashioned, but there was something special about going to the mailbox and holding an actual invitation. I had them professionally designed, and the top of the invitation read:

Shh! This is a Roundup

(... and not her first rodeo!)

An image of a pink and blue felt hat was underneath the heading with thin leather strings hanging from the hats as straps. Indeed, that would have been perfect for both girls, too. An invitation was also mailed to Lily, but she never mentioned that she had received it. My concern was that she would leave it lying around and Sadie might notice it but thought it best to not put any ideas in her head. Her jealousy had clearly accelerated to an uncomfortable level and in a deviant way, she might be prone to spoil the surprise.

Memorial Weekend arrived and all of us were low-key, especially with Sadie entering her ninth month of pregnancy. There had been a few occasions when all of us were together and thank the heavens that Lily stopped wearing the maternity clothes. How awkward would that have been for her to stroll into Sadie's shower looking pregnant?

On Sunday at ten o'clock Lily and I taxied over to Suzie's to bring everything for the shower. The restaurant graciously allowed us to enter an hour prior to when they opened. I confirmed the number of people and reviewed the menu one last time.

"Sep, you can go on ahead. I'm going to set up the room upstairs since it's reserved. You're welcome to help but I know you'll want to shower and get ready."

"What about you, Lily? I can't leave you with all of this to set up."

One of the wait staff interjected. "We aren't busy here so I'm happy to help organize the upstairs. We're good at this and have assisted with so many parties."

I wanted to do my own micromanaging but the situation, given that two people were already on top of it, didn't lend itself to my being there. Besides, I did want to go home to get ready.

"Very well, then. I'll call the bakery and double-check that they'll deliver here by noon."

"Done, Sep. Check, check."

Lily had totally stepped up.

CHAPTER 24

Cowboy or Cowgirl?

I arrived at Suzie's Wild West on the Upper West at 2:30 to greet our guests arriving close to three o'clock. Josh would be bringing Sadie at 3:15ish and Wes and Adam planned to join us later.

Lily was sitting in the bar area having a cocktail and was dressed for the occasion. She had gone home to change and was wearing jeans with a plaid button-down shirt, short shoe boots, and a western belt.

"Hey, cowgirl! Thank you for setting up. I'm excited to see the room."

"My pleasure." Lily signaled the bartender. "I'll have another to take upstairs with me. Do you want to have a drink?"

"No, no. I'm fine."

The bartender handed Lily another martini and she stood up, grabbed another napkin, and motioned me to follow her.

"Shall we?"

I trailed behind her up the flight of stairs and she pushed open the wooden saloon doors to the private party room.

My jaw dropped!

Lily had transformed the room into the perfect western baby shower! I realized then that I'd been unkind in my thoughts about her. Deep down inside she was clearly thrilled for Sadie and today she had unequivocally done justice to the event.

"You like?"

"I love!"

Lily had left no stone unturned. The table centerpieces were made from fake tumbleweed underneath baby books that had a western theme. Next to each place setting, Lily had ordered drinking glasses shaped like boots with a baby charm hanging from their handles, and the bandanas were used as napkins. The felt hats hung off each chair. Against the wall a long table was set up for the gifts with a sign that read, "Put a fork in her, she's done! Add your words of wisdom for baby #2 into the jar." Slips of paper with brown edges were in a pile with pens that had a sheriff's badge at the top.

"I hope Sadie likes all of this?"

"Oh, she will, Lily. Whenever she visits this restaurant, she dresses up western. So, please don't think that she knows about the shower."

"Being nine months pregnant, though, she'll probably just wear a big-ass maternity dress."

Really?

Lily exceeded my expectations with planning the shower, but I certainly hadn't needed that last comment. After twenty minutes passed, our guests began to arrive. Everyone decided to dress for a themed party. Sadie's friends were somethin' else, all beautiful and creative women inside and out! As I greeted each girl I noticed from the corner of my eye Lily ordering another martini from the waitress as she held up her empty glass.

The maître d' signaled us twenty minutes after three that Sadie had arrived. We all quieted.

The saloon doors opened several minutes later and there stood Sadie looking magnificent! It was not some big-ass maternity dress but only God knew how she had found the sexiest, ripped, white maternity jeans to wear with her white Lucchese boots. On the top was a brown, low-cut leather halter that spread out over the top of her jeans to the top of her thighs. Around her neck, a white and turquoise bolo necklace hung into her cleavage. I'd never seen a pregnant woman look sexier! Elle had worn almost an identical outfit and there was so much pride on Josh's face.

I started to become concerned with the amount of alcohol that Lily was consuming and knew I would feel more at ease if both Wes and Adam were here. When Lily was brought another cocktail, I walked over to her.

"How are you doing, Lily? Please, come over and greet everyone. I certainly want you to take credit for organizing this beautiful baby sprinkle."

Her eyes looked a little glassy.

"I'm okay, but I don't like what I'm wearing."

"Oh, pea, it's perfect for this party!"

And ... I see it coming. Please don't have me babysit her personality today. I can't stabilize her after my daughter has just walked in and is a showstopper. Sadie owns a room each and every time, and I'm not going to apologize for that.

"Lily, should I ask Adam to come here a little earlier? Is

there something else from home that he can bring you that you'd want to wear?"

"No, let me just sit for a while and have my drink."

I walked over to Sadie and whispered that she should spend a few minutes with Lily.

"Lily put this entire shower together, Sadie, and I think she's feeling sad. You know, the loss of her baby. She's unhappy with what she's wearing and is consuming too much alcohol. I'm sorry."

"No problem. Let me handle it."

Sadie walked over to Lily.

"Lily, you're the best sister anyone can ask for. Mom said that you did *all of this!*" Sadie opened her arms wide and spun around as if to introduce the room. "Come with me. I want you to meet some friends who you may not know. Let me show you off!"

Lily stood from the table.

"Lily, you can leave the drink on the table." Sadie put the cocktail napkin on top of the glass. "It will still be here. The napkin on the top tells the waitress not to take it away."

Lily complied and Sadie held her hand.

She seemed to be holding it together as Sadie included her in conversations while appetizers were passed around.

Forty-five minutes passed and Wes showed up, then Adam shortly thereafter. We had a small "guys table" set up in the corner. My son, Jack, had promised to make his appearance at some point, but this was totally not his thing, he had said. I grew more relaxed knowing that Adam was now here to tame Lily. She continued to drink but I noticed that Adam extracted himself from having that conversation with her so as to not create a scene. I was observant; this, I knew, was the beginning of the end of their marriage.

Everyone seated themselves to be served lunch and Sadie stood up to make a small speech. Elle followed her.

"A warm and delicious welcome to my friends, family, and our special men in the room."

At that moment, Jack arrived.

"Just in time, Bro! Making your grand entrance, as always!"

Jack smiled and walked over to hug his sister.

"This is a special time for our family and especially Elly, who will soon have a brother or sister."

"It will be Cecilia or Drew," shouted Elle. "And Drew is *not* short for Andrew, Mommy said!"

"Thank you for sharing, Elly. Everyone knows the names we picked and thank you for reminding us it is not short for Andrew."

"You're welcome!" Elle said as she hugged Sadie's belly.

"Lily arranged this beautiful, themed party and left no stone unturned when pulling everything together."

"And G-Sep, too!"

"Yes, Elly, I'm getting to that. Sep and Lily, I could not imagine a better team to make this happen. This is our favorite place and a perfect gathering place for our well-wishers. Josh, would you like to say anything?"

"No, dear. You and Elly have it covered!" he called out from the table.

Everyone laughed.

"Sep?"

"Say something, G-Sep!" Elle called out.

"Okay, Elly. I'm so grateful that our family continues to expand and deliver the kind of love to each other that keeps us solid. And all of you here, Sadie's friends, your unconditional caring and friendship promotes the same solid foundation outside of this family circle. Wait! We are all one big circle!" I laughed.

Sadie lifted her water glass. "And let's toast!"

"We're not quite finished with the toasts, are we?" Lily walked up to Sadie.

"Absolutely not, Lily. You have the floor. Please." Sadie stepped aside.

"I'm not sure if everyone knows this, but Elle would be having a baby girl cousin if Baby T hadn't died in my belly. Baby T, for Tessa, named after my mother. I had to deliver a stillborn after six months."

The room silenced. You could have heard a pin drop.

Elle ran over to Josh and crawled onto his lap.

Adam rose from his chair.

"Sit down, Adam. I'm fine. I'm very happy for Sadie and Josh and Elle, and obviously Sep and Wes. I so wished that I could have contributed to growing this family with a baby of my own now that I am part of this family."

"We all love you," said Sadie and gave her a hug.

The waitress rang a little bell to announce that lunch was being served. Saved by the bell!

I sat down and looked over at Adam. He caught my stare and shook his head. Lily took her seat next to me and our table was silent. My food could barely get past the lump in my throat.

Elle ran back to our table.

"What a wonderful baby sprinkle! Don't you all agree?" blurted Lily.

"It sure is!" Elle said and sat between me and Sadie.

When lunch ended it was approaching five o'clock, time to

open gifts. Lily took the reins on this.

"Sadie, come sit in this chair next to the gifts, please. Sep, can you write down whom each gift is from? There should be a pad of paper and a pen in the bag next to you."

"Yes," I said. "Got it!"

"But before we open the gifts, I have a special surprise!"

Lily walked over to the corner of the room and carried over an easel with a fabric blanket depicting a covered wagon covering it. Quite frankly, I had thought it was part of the room's décor.

"We can't have a baby sprinkle without a themed sign-in board. Do we agree?"

Lily pulled up the bottom corners of the blanket, over the top of the easel, and revealed a large cardboard sign.

"Ta-da! My special shower gift to Sadie!"

No one in the room moved. My poor daughter's face had a look of horror.

Lily uncovered a "WANTED" poster framed in black with brown edges, similar to what you'd see nailed to a tree during the late 1800s. There were two separate pictures, side by side on the cardboard, a baby boy and a baby girl with the names "DREW" and "CECILIA" below them. And across the board in large, bold black letters:

WANTED: DEAD OR ALIVE

C H A P T E R 2 5

The Showdown

Sadie cupped her hands around the sides of her belly and looked down. Slowly she lifted her head and her eyes pierced through Lily's, while Lily turned up the corners of her mouth in a grin. If Sadie could breathe fire, she'd have burned her at the stake.

"Wasn't that creative, Sadie? Sadie, Sadie, fancy lady?"

"Adam," Sadie called across the room, "would you mind calling a taxi for Lily? She told me earlier that she wasn't feeling well, and I think it's best that she goes home."

Sadie turned back to Lily. "Thank you for planning this beautiful shower with Sep and you've already done way too much. We'll save some of the dessert for you, okay?"

"I'm feeling quite well. There's no reason for me to leave."

"Let's gather your things, dear. I'm taking you home," implored Adam.

"I'm not going anywhere with you." Lily forcefully pulled

her arm out of his grasp.

"Lily," Sadie said in a calm and controlled tone, "how about you and I go downstairs and have a chat while dessert is served?"

Josh stood up from his chair as I began walking over to intervene.

"It ends here." Wes belted out in a pitch that jolted the room. "Right here, right now. Lily, you need to leave, with or without Adam. This is not a circus performance for our friends and family, and it won't be conducted as such. Take your horse and pony show somewhere else. Do all of us a favor and get the hell out."

Lily stood motionless.

"You heard me, move! Or I'll haul your damn ass out myself!"

"Josh," Wes then called in a calm voice, "kindly take this easel out of the room."

Josh complied, allowing Wes to take the lead on the situation.

Adam ushered Lily through the saloon doors, then turned to look back into the room.

"Apologies to everyone here. My wife is not well."

Adam and Lily disappeared, but what had transpired was too traumatizing for anyone still present to enjoy the last hour of Sadie's baby sprinkle.

"Mommy," squeaked Elle in a soft, frightened tone, "in school the teacher makes one big circle, and everyone has a chance to share something."

"Oh, Elly, that's the best idea. Let's do it. Each person can share their gift with me," said Sadie, who then commissioned the guys to push the tables to the sides of the room and made a full circle with the chairs.

"Mommy's chair has to be in the middle. And one for G-Sep."

I sat in the chair next to my daughter with Elle on the floor between us.

"Okay, Elly, show us what to do."

Elle asked each person who had brought a gift to hand it to her mother. Once the gift was opened, one after the other, the friend shared why they chose the gift.

I recorded each gift and the waitress walked around the circle with the tray of cookies and cupcakes. Once the dessert was served to each guest, my granddaughter walked away from the circle and chased down the tray. Typical!

"Elle, come back here," I called out to her. "G-Sep and Wes have a present for you!"

She ran back to us faster than her legs could carry her. "What is it? What is it?"

"Well, first, this is for Mommy." Wes brought over the little velvet pouch with the bracelet I had bought for her for Valentine's Day at Abracadabra on Lex.

"A sterling silver bracelet with a pearl charm, the June birthstone for a June baby. I love it, Sep," Sadie breathed.

"I'm so glad, honey. Let me put it on your wrist."

"Where's my present, G-Sep?" Elle demanded.

Wes handed Elle her gift and she attacked the wrapping paper to uncover a magic wand.

"A real wand! Look, Mommy, I can do magic!"

"Elle, you can wave it over Mommy's belly and wish for either a baby brother or a baby sister," I said.

"Oh, G-Sep, can I also wish for Baby T to come out, too? I'm supposed to get a cousin, too. Remember?"

"Elly, girl," explained Sadie, "only one baby will come out and it will be your brother or sister. Okay?"

Elle waved the wand over her mother's belly.

"Okay. Abracadabra. Abracadabra. I wish for ... Cecilia, my baby sister. Come out soon."

Everyone clapped and Elle took a bow.

"Elly, we shall call her Cece!" Sadie loves Cece as a nickname.

The men began packing up the gifts into large bags and left it to our little spitfire to save the day.

Hugs, and words of appreciation were given to all our guests. Elle handed out a cowboy hat for everyone to take home and said, "Happy trails."

"Happy trails, to you. Happy trails, to you. Happy trails to you ..." Elle sang on repeat.

After the fifteenth time we were all ready to throw her tiny ass and big mouth into a covered wagon and send her on her way. She was as cute as a button but contained non-stop energy!

Wes and I arrived home close to 6:30 and were completely exhausted. No words were spoken about the Lily fiasco, but no doubt Adam had his hands full.

"Wes, do you think I should text Adam?"

"No, he needs to sort this out and you need to relax. I'm sorry if I overstepped my bounds but I've been watching Lily turn things upside down for quite some time and my priority is you, Sadie, and Elle. I will never allow anyone to hurt my girls."

"I swear. I don't know what I've done to deserve a man like you."

"I'm far from perfect."

"But you're perfect for me."

Wes lifted me up and carried me in his arms.

"You just enticed this ol' cowboy so now you're getting lassoed into the bed."

I grabbed one of the powder-blue felt cowboy hats off the table and put it on my head.

"Save a horse, ride a cowboy!"

"Wes, you nasty, nasty, cowboy."

"I'm jumping in for a quick shower. Care to join me?"

"I think I like that idea. Go on ahead of me."

Wes was the gentlest man in every way, but today his claws had come out. In that harrowing moment he had taken control and put an end to the madness. A gentle giant, he was, but his emotional fortitude and unwavering convictions made him sexy as hell. Though he was behaving as cool as a cucumber, I knew him well, and he was concerned that he had overstepped. The tiger in him had me so sexually stimulated. How fucked up was that, coming off the heels of such an unsettling afternoon?

When I heard Wes pull the shower door shut, I went directly to my closet and pulled out something I had purchased weeks ago from Cosabella to save for our wedding night. There seemed to be unexpected surprises around every corner and now I was all about living in the moment. Our oversized walk-in closet was perfect for my costume change.

When the shower turned off, Wes called out from the bathroom, "You disappointed me, cowgirl. Why didn't you join me?"

I giggled.

The bathroom door opened, and steam escaped, then Wes emerged.

"Where are you?"

"Grrrr," I growled and crawled out of the closet on my hands and knees with my right arm stretched out in front of me and my left leg stretched back.

Wes stood there in amazement. He dropped the towel from his waist, and he hung beautifully. I prowled toward him, knees brushing across the carpet.

My breasts spilled slightly over the top of the white bralette, and I looked up at him like a naughty girl. The sheer lace white garter skirt with thigh-highs attached to its straps fit nicely over the matching thong. They clung to my body as I crawled toward him, my head down while looking up at him. It was this seductive thing that I do.

"Throw me on the bed and play with me, Wesley. Have your way."

"No, no bed. Tigresses don't do it in the comfort of a bed."

He walked in back of me and got down on the floor, positioning his body on top of mine while I remained on all fours.

"Prop up that magnificent ass, nice and high."

I felt the warmth of his tongue licking the small of my back while he squeezed my right breast and then allowed it to fall out of its cup. His hand traveled to my buttocks, lifted the skirt, and then moved the thong to one side. Teasingly he bit me, and it hurt in a good way, filling me with anticipated excitement. And with aggression he entered me hard.

"Wes, I'd rah ... rather b ... be your whore th ... than anybody else's wah ... wife," I said in a staccato as he pounded me rhythmically with my hair wound up in the palm of his hand.

"Love, you will be both."

My body weakened and I laid face down on the carpet, abandoning any inclination for self-control. My provocation invited him to invade my body in ways that were sacrilegious. He was close, close to the pinnacle and I could feel his saliva dripping down my cheek; he was losing his shit, losing his mind.

"Damn you, girl! What have you done to me?" He struggled to get the words out.

"Slow. Slow down, cowboy. Don't let go. Not just yet."

He started to pull back, but I could tell he was about to cross the threshold.

"I can't ...."

"Yes, you can."

"Please ..."

"I'll tell you when. Don't fuck with me."

"Okay, I'm trying."

"How bad do you want to let go?"

"Oh, so bad, real bad ..."

"I'll tell you when, cowboy ... wait ... wait ..."

His thrusts brought me to the edge, where I wanted both of us to be.

"Are you ready now, cowboy?"

"Yeah, I'm letting go."

He was rigid, tight, and snug as a bug in a rug.

"... and I'm with you."

He slowed the thrusts and then pulled my buttocks in tight to him, holding us in a stationary position. Our breathing became shallow, and his throbbing went from swells to ripples. We were crazed and in love, like disobedient teenagers fucking in the backseat of our parents' car. I panted quietly and he nuzzled his face in my nest of hair. Neither of us moved.

Wes' breathing carried a tempo and I dozed off to what became a melody, our melody. Lying lifeless between the carpet and the heaviness of his body I dreamt that we became one soul.

CHAPTER 26

Lily Unravels

The sun peeked through the bedroom window and granted us another blessed day.

Wes and I crawled into our bed at daybreak for another few hours of sleep. My body ached from sleeping on the floor, Wes on top of me, the wool Berber branding blotchy circles on my right cheek and temple. I continued to dream while snuggled up in Wes' arms, but unsettling images of distorted babies kept me restless, a reminder that reality was waiting to smack me in the head when I began the day.

I planned to camp out at Sadie's place to sort through her shower gifts and tease out yesterday's troubling event. A massive cleanup was needed to unpack everyone's distress from Lily's performance. She had become the undertow with the ability to languish our family's ship, the catalyst for all good things to turn sour with her unpredictable behavior in any setting. She was not the girl I once knew, and the foundation that

I had tried to help her establish seemed to be cracking.

My undergarments were strewn on the floor along with Wes' damp towel. After picking up the remains of last night's steamy episode of debauchery, I showered and allowed Wes to continue sleeping peacefully. And with my morning coffee, I had half of a bagel with a side of numerous missed phone calls from Lily. Amongst the litany of missed calls was a text from Adam.

My apologies for Lily's behavior and wish I could undo the unthinkable. I'm at a loss. Not going to burden you with phone calls. Stayed in a hotel last night and will return to the apartment later today once I've had time to collect my thoughts.

When I finished reading the text I began listening to Lily's messages. They started out somewhat benign but progressed to placing blame on Adam, then feeling distraught about the loss of her baby, then asking if she could stay with Wes and me. Because I hadn't returned any of the phone calls her messages became increasingly more aggressive and self-deprecating. She ranted about her mother leaving her and then over the fact that Adam would leave her. She positioned me as being next in line and bringing my family along for the ride. Lily was driving down the road of self-destruction, and Wes had a low threshold for tolerating her shenanigans. At that point, I almost need to lie to him by omission.

I stepped out onto the terrace to return Adam's call, but it went to voicemail.

"Hey, Adam, please don't ever feel like you can't call me. We're all in this together and you're a part of our family. Call when you can."

When I walked back inside, I could hear Wes beginning to stir, a signal he'd be getting out of bed.

Sadie's call was coming in.

"Hey," I answered with an upward inflection.

"Hey, Sep."

"Did you sleep well? I'm planning to come over today if you're still up to it."

"I'd like that. Josh will be taking Elly out for the day. She was sifting through the shower gifts and walking around with the unopened toys, pouting, of course. We're going to allow her to shop to her heart's content at the toy store."

"Sounds like a plan. Wes will be up shortly, and I'll have coffee with him before I head over to you."

"Later, gator."

Wes snuck up behind me and teasingly bit me on the neck.

"Wifey, what the hell was *that* all about? Last night? Holy smokestacks!"

"I know, right? I had this sick thought. Imagine if we croaked during sex and the kids found us like that?"

"That is pretty depraved. Who was on the phone?"

"Oh, I'm going over to Sadie's to help organize her shower gifts."

Wes stood there with his eyebrows raised.

"What?" I asked.

"You know what."

"I really don't."

"Look, I know you like I know the back of my hand. There's not a chance in hell that Lily won't make it into a part of your day. Have you heard from her yet?"

"Adam texted me that he slept in a hotel. Lily left me a dozen or so voice messages."

"Honey, this has to end. She needs the kind of help that none of us can give her. Adam has his hands full, but he is her husband. She's a married woman and they'll have to figure this thing out as a couple. I know you want to be her savior but you're treading in dangerous waters."

"I know, I know, I know," I responded, holding my hands over my ears. "It's just so hard."

Wes moved in close, held me tight, and whispered, "Go enjoy your daughter."

I arrived at Sadie's shortly past 11:30 and I decided to make a concerted effort to extract myself from my phone, though the million backlogged calls from Lily were weighing heavily on me. It was mind-boggling how I'd allowed her to rent space in my head.

Elle tugged on me the second I walked in the door, and behind her, Sadie was bringing out a pot of brewed coffee.

"Let's go, little princess! We're off to the toy store!" Josh scooped her up and then leaned in to give me a kiss on the cheek.

"You gals have some serious business here today. We'll see you later!"

I was overjoyed to have this time with Sadie.

"Sit, Sep. I also baked muffins."

She and I made small talk but clearly there was an elephant in the room. I knew she sensed my edginess, and so badly I wanted her to mention Lily.

"Sep, I was graced with so many nice gifts, but some have to be returned. Elly has tons of books and toys that I put away. I must say that the *best* gift was a sound machine. I never had one of those darn things for Elly, but they make sense."

"Well, let's go through everything and make piles."

My phone started buzzing.

"Hi, Wes, I just got here. Do you miss me already?"

"You know I do, but listen, Lily just stopped by our apartment."

"What?"

"She said she left you numerous messages and thought your phone might be off."

"So, what did you tell her?

"I told her you weren't home, but I'd give you the message. She looked bad."

"What do you mean?"

"A bit crazed and disheveled. I asked her if she wanted to talk for a few minutes, but she spewed some venomous comments my way, angered that I asked her to leave the shower."

"Oh, boy. Well, I'm putting my phone away so I can enjoy a few peaceful hours here."

"Sounds like a plan."

"Now what? Another debacle?" questioned Sadie, rolling her eyes.

"Lily stopped by the apartment."

"She's become an impossible situation, Sep, and Adam needs to get her under control. Lily is unraveling and it's sad to see, but she's stressing everyone out."

"Adam didn't sleep at home last night."

"Great, that's just great. Now we have an undiagnosed lunatic on the loose."

Before I could say another word, Sadie made a hand motion dismissing further conversation about her. As if yesterday wasn't enough, now she was just fed up, and I didn't want to push her.

After having my third cup of coffee of the day and bouncing off the walls, I moved over to the sofa with Sadie to sort through the gifts.

"It feels so amazing to have my alone time with you and to prepare for Grandbaby Cecilia or Drew's arrival. And it seems like it was just yesterday when we were waiting for Elle to make her grand entrance."

"I'm glad we didn't do a reveal," Sadie said. "There are so few occasions in life when we can be surprised."

A heavy knock on the door interrupted our conversation.

"Coming, coming," she called out. "Jesus, who the hell can this be?"

"Honey, I'll get up."

"No, I'm good."

Sadie pulled herself up, holding her belly, to answer the door.

"Yes?"

"It's me. Lily. Open the door." Her voice was loud and impatient.

"Oh, Lily. Look, I'm alone here and just jumping into the shower. Can I call you later?"

"Can I come in and wait? I really need to talk to you."

"This isn't a good time. Let me call you later, okay?"

"Well, have you heard from Seppie? I've been trying to reach her all day." Lily's tone now sounded angry and upset.

I snapped my fingers to catch Sadie's attention and nodded.

"No, sorry, Lily. I haven't."

"Right. You haven't heard from your mother. Not once today? Yeah."

"I'll let her know you're trying to reach her if I speak with her, okay?"

No response.

"Okay, Lily?"

Dead silence.

Sadie turned to me and threw her hands up in the air, shaking her head.

She and I returned to the gifts. I thought I heard something outside the apartment, then tiptoed over to the door. When I looked through the peephole there was an eye staring back at me, and I nearly shit my pants!

Sadie saw me jump and I signaled her to be quiet with my finger in front of my lips. Sadie's eyes opened wide.

I went over and whispered in her ear, "She's standing at the door."

Fifteen minutes later when I checked, she was sitting at the bottom of the staircase.

"What the actual fuck, Sadie? She's sitting in the stairwell?"

"Let's call Wes. I don't want to call Josh. This is his day with Elle."

When I walked into the bedroom to call Wes, thinking he should come over, Sadie told me she was no longer there. We left it at that, and I put the phone down. She and I continued with our visit, with or without Lily's presence, I felt a storm approaching.

At 3:30, Josh returned with Elle with bags of God knew what! He made no mention that he saw Lily skulking around, so presumably she never returned.

"Love you all but I have to head back home," said Seppie.

"Sep, would you like Josh to walk you out?" Sadie raised her eyebrows, and I knew what she was asking me.

"I'm good," I told her.

"Stay, G-Sep?" begged Elle.

"Honey, show Mommy all your presents and I'll see you on another day. Come here, give me a hug!"

Elle gave me the biggest squeeze and I thought about how

great it would be if things were uncomplicated. Lily was over-whelming all of us, whether she realized it or not.

A Bad Moon is Rising

And the drama continued. An hour after I returned home Adam called.

"Hi, Seppie, is Wes with you?"

"Yes, why?"

"Can you put me on speaker?"

"Sure, what's happening?" I motioned Wes to come over to the phone.

"This is more of a heads up that Lily is quickly accelerating to a bad place," Adam began.

Wes and I looked at each other intently.

"As both of you know, I didn't sleep at home last night. But when I returned this afternoon Lily had destroyed a lot of things in our apartment. The glass on our framed wedding pictures were smashed and my suits were pulled from the wardrobe with pockets turned inside out. You get the description. She called me a liar and a cheat, and then went on to say that you're ignoring her and we're in some sort of conspiracy."

Once Adam stopped to take a breath, I interjected, detailing the escapades that had occurred at Sadie's place. My intent was not to stoke the fire but to expose the severity of Lily's irrational behavior, which warranted professional attention.

"Really?" said Wes with a confused look. "You didn't call me?"

No doubt I would endure Wes' wrath for this one.

"Lily stood by the door, then eventually sat at the bottom of the stairs. After some time, she left so I thought it was fine."

Wes looked down and shook his head.

"I'm sorry. I should have—"

"Look," said Adam, "you have nothing to feel badly about. She has taken a toll on all of us. It turned ugly here today with her hitting me uncontrollably to the point I had to call the police. There are visible scratch marks on my face and my arms. I'm considering a restraining order. This hurts me so much. I told her I would pay for a hotel until she can make other arrangements. She's not in a good emotional space right now and all of us need to be on guard."

"So, we don't know where she went?"

"The police stayed here while she gathered her belongings, then escorted her out. The entire time she fussed about how I repeatedly verbally and physically abused her, and her attacking me was in self-defense. No one can make this up. All of you have your lives to live but I'm just keeping you informed that this is a bad situation."

"How can Seppie and I help?"

"Thank you, Wes. I'm trying to figure this out. Just stay on alert and share this information with Sadie, Josh, and Jack."

"I'm so sorry, Adam. For all this agony."

"It's not anyone's fault. I'm moving back to Wisconsin and ending our lease at the end of the month. The lease is in my name, and I may have to change the locks. I have a pulse on positions in other law firms, and it's in my best interest to leave New York. I'll miss all of you terribly but know that you understand the predicament here."

"Of course, we do," Wes and I said in unison.

"Be careful, Adam, and we'll be in touch with each other," I said with wishful thinking.

"Love you guys."

"We love you, too," I said before disconnecting.

Wes didn't get annoyed often, but his stern look had me so upset. I could feel the perspiration being absorbed by my shirt fabric.

"I know. I know I should have called you."

"What am I going to do with you? This is bad and you don't see it, do you?"

"Wait, sorry, Wes. Sadie's calling. Hi, Sadie. Yes, I'm okay and sorry that I forgot to call you when I got home."

"Please put Sadie on speaker," Wes said curtly.

"Sadie, you're on speaker. Wes is—"

"Hey, Sadie. Look, your mother is going to be angry with me, but she needs to sever this relationship with Lily. Adam just called. Lily destroyed the apartment and became physical with him. The police were called and stayed while she packed her bags. He will need to change the locks. I am gravely concerned."

Sadie sent me a FaceTime request, and I accepted.

"Both of you, hold on here," I said, "I cannot continue to ignore her. Not returning her calls will only escalate her behavior and the truth is that she needs help."

"I do agree with that," Wes said, "but the only way to face this is head-on," Wes puffed. "Please, help me out here, Sadie."

"Let me be clear here, Mom, and you know how much I've always loved Lily."

She never called me mom.

"This charade has to end. This *will* end and Lily will be made to understand that the dynamics between her and our family are no longer healthy ... which means, we can no longer be available to her. If she *doesn't* get it, well, that's just too friggin' bad. While we cannot control *her* behavior, we have control over our decisions moving forward. This, unfortunately, is the culmination of every one of her destructive episodes. What we have here is the tail wagging the dog."

"That sounds logical, Sadie, but she has no one. No one! Where will she go? And I feel like all of us will be on edge just waiting to bump into her somewhere, like a rabid dog on the loose."

"You just said it," interjected Wes. "I didn't. A rabid dog on the loose. Is this really what you're okay with?"

"No, no! The two of you are haranguing me."

My brain hurt, cluttered with having to defend myself. I didn't appreciate being pushed into a corner.

"I'm doing the best I can, but I can't be okay with abandoning this child in her worst moments. A girl—"

"Damn it, Sep, she's no longer a child! Cut the shit. Cut your losses here. She is a troubled young woman who's unsteady and scary and we have become her prey. She has crossed the line and no longer has rights when she's infringing on ours. You're afraid to 'poke the bear' but all of us will continue to be targets of her fury, regardless."

Sadie had clearly lost her patience with me and was hormonal, I was sure, getting ready to drop this next baby.

"Honey, listen," said Wes in a calm voice. "We know that you are selfless and sympathetic to a fault. It's those qualities that we love about you, but you can't fix this. You cannot jeopardize the safety and stability of this family."

"Sep, I'm ready to have this baby and, oh, please … look, the fact that Adam is contemplating an Order of Protection shows that she is unpredictably vicious."

"Perhaps I can ease the blow of the conversation with Lily by telling her we'll always leave the door open for her to return once she gets the help that—"

"No, no, no. This can never work in your favor!" Sadie now raised her voice. "I don't understand what *you* don't understand about the gravity of this situation?"

"Let's do this, Seppie. I have a thought," said Wes. "If and when, and I'm certain that she will, Lily reaches out to you, I will go with you to meet her in a public place. Together, we'll have a conversation with her and broach the subject of her getting some help. She has had a lot of trauma in her life and our conversation will come from a place of concern and caring. If she doesn't take the bait and refuses, then this chapter has to close in a way that she won't feel angry with you about. Does that make sense? You've been a part of her life for a long time and if you don't have proper closure, you won't be able to rest with this. This much I know."

"Wes," said Sadie, "I'm not certain that meeting her at all is a sound decision."

"I totally understand your feeling that way, but you and I both know your mother very well. She will ruminate about this. And both of us know that for your mom, it is like letting go of a daughter.”

“I know you’re right about that, Wes, and I have taken her in like a sister. But, you can’t expect me to watch Lily continue to hurt the people who love her.”

“Listen to the two of you,” I said. “I’m not a child. I don’t need an intervention.”

“Uh, but you do,” Sadie said in a snarky tone. “I won’t stand by and have Lily disrupt your life. Hey, I’m getting off the phone now to settle in and then getting to sleep early tonight. I have nothing left in me, Sep. I hope you take to heart what we’re telling you without being defensive. We love you. Hugs. Night, Wes.”

“Night, night, Sadie.”

Sadie ended the call and Wes pulled me in close. I sobbed and held onto him like a life raft.

“You’ll be all right, honey. You will. When any of us are so embroiled in a relationship it’s hard to see the fruit from the trees, sometimes. And as much as you tirelessly try to right Lily’s wrongs, in the end she’s responsible for her actions. You’ll let go of her emotionally when you’re ready but keeping her physically connected gives her the leeway to continually sabotage the good. Lily may not have hit her rock bottom, because when that happens, she’ll figure out how to pull herself out of the trenches.”

I lifted my face up, leaving black mascara smudges on Wes’ shirt.

“How are you so smart, Mr. Harlow?”

“Because I chose you to be my wife?”

A day passed, then two, and then a week. Lily never reached out to me again. Perhaps no one else realized it, but her silence kept the door open. Should she surface, and should Wes and

I meet with her, my well-rehearsed parting speech would be delivered like an amateur actor. My words would feel forced and empty because the thought of ushering her away to get swallowed up in the universe would leave me feeling guilty. On their wedding day I made a promise to her mother that I would carry out her role in her absence. How was I supposed to come to terms with breaking that promise to care for her daughter?

Lily might have believed that I abandoned her because I stopped responding, and that was why she was no longer reaching out to me. Or was she silently forging a plan of attack? The Lily we knew had a different look and my struggle to let go of the past was on me. It was my problem. Letting go had always been my challenge in relationships, waiting for the other person to unhandcuff me.

I moved through each day not mentioning Lily's name while enjoying Sadie and waiting for our "special delivery." Her bag was packed and ready to accompany her to the hospital. I'd busied myself with buying special treats for Elle to prepare her for when much attention would be given to her sibling. There was a sense of peace, enjoying family time without disruption. Until I began thinking about that loose end.

Ironically, I stayed glued to my phone, waiting for the gaggle of geese like I waited for Teddy's call after we'd first met. It felt interesting to make that analogy. I'd had no closure with Lily.

CHAPTER 28

The Family Nest: One In and One Out

Adam accepted a position in Wisconsin at Spencer, Spencer, and Wake, a firm specializing in environmental law, with the opportunity to make partner in the firm. Relocating back to his Midwestern roots seemed like a logical choice since his mother had been battling some medical issues. Though she had a cadre of friends, the move would keep him close by and Adam could reconnect with childhood friends who had remained in Madison. He needed a fresh start.

In the throes of a tumultuous divorce, it was costing Adam a pretty penny, but leaving it in the hands of a well-established divorce attorney helped free him from Lily's clutches, which had proved a financial drain and an emotional slaughterhouse. Her irredeemable and reprehensible behavior accelerated to mammoth proportions, and a restraining order was put into place.

Our concerted effort to assist Adam during this transition

had sparked Lily's desperation to sneak back under the covers in our family bed by making accusations that we had deserted her and that we owed her another chance to redeem herself. I did try to call her and left a message, hoping we could meet, but she neither answered nor returned the call.

Lily had begun blowing up Sadie's and Wes' phones with messages and they both blocked her number. It felt as though we were plugging up the holes of a leak but each time, Lily's water spouted from another place as she tried to divide and conquer, manipulating us individually to give her another chance. Her perseverance to invade my family's emotional space extricated a lot of the enjoyment we derived from just "living our lives." She'd essentially become untamable.

The offer that Wes had made for us to meet her in a public place expired, for obvious reasons, and I didn't dare to push that envelope. Lily had not reached out to me, so I hadn't blocked her number. I felt alienated from her, the way she'd likely felt by me.

"G-Sep, help me figure out this puzzle," Elle demanded, looking frustrated.

"Okay, pumpkin." I lifted myself off the sofa, next to Sadie, and walked over to the center of the living room where Elle is playing.

"Sweetheart, this is a very hard puzzle!"

My phone began vibrating in my pocket.

Jeez, it's Lily calling.

Sadie was sitting on the sofa with her feet up, and my heart was pounding out of my chest because I wanted to hear Lily's voice. This couldn't have been worse timing.

"Hello," I answered in a whisper.

"I lost my job. I lost my husband and baby. I need help,"

Lily sobbed.

I dropped my voice below a whisper. "Oh, Lily, I …"

"Oh, Lily? Oh, Lily what?!"

"Please don't think that—" I began to say.

"How unfortunate, very unfortunate that I couldn't be Sadie." Her tone turned angry. "And that Sadie couldn't be in my shitty position. Let's count. There are two children for her and none for me, a mother for Sadie and none for me."

I stepped aside so Sadie wouldn't be in earshot of our conversation.

"That's unfair of you to say," I retorted, trying to defend myself. "My family and I embraced …"

"G-Sep, it's your turn to go," Elle called out.

I placed my fingers over my lips to shush Elle, and she went back to playing by herself.

"You damn motherfuckers don't give a shit about what happens to me! I'm not heartless like my father, that heartless pig! I am *not* my father!"

"No one thinks you are anything like—"

"Lily, you're just like a sister. Lily, you're a daughter to me," she said in a sardonic tone, mimicking Sadie and me. "All of you have moved on. Shame on *all* of you."

I stood speechless with the phone pressed tightly to my ear. Empty. I had no words. I could see why she felt abandoned.

Lily jockeyed between sobbing and then yelling obscenities, her pendulum swinging violently. She was a broken girl at the brink of a nervous breakdown, her words making no sense.

"Holy umph! Is that Lily screaming on the phone?" Sadie asked sharply, not wanting to curse in front of Elle. The fire in her eyes could have set the room ablaze.

"Sadie, I didn't …" I stammered, trying to mute the phone

so Sadie wouldn't hear.

"Oh, we have Sadie in the room? Hey, hey, Sadie in the house!" Lily began laughing.

"You didn't what? You didn't call her? Sep, you picked up her phone call!"

Sadie shuffled over, standing akimbo in front of me. She stared, then held out her hand. "The phone!"

I began retracting my arm, but she reached out and snatched the phone, then shut it down.

"We're done with this crap. Done."

Sadie's disappointment in me was the worst punishment I could have ever received. I was torn between wanting to let go of Lily and wanting to be Lily's savior even at the cost of Sadie taking on the role of being my responsible parent. And that was fucked up, now that I thought about it. Had I completely lost my mind?

We settled back down on the sofa and Sadie commissioned Elle to play on her own for a while. She blocked Lily's number from my phone and then discussed an Order of Protection for all of us.

"We must do this, Sep. Please. We are done."

Sadie and I sat together for a very long time, and she held my hand. Both of us knew what the other was thinking, and I appreciated that my daughter allowed me the dignity to redeem my behavior.

"Sep, we'll inform Josh and Wes that we have come to the decision of securing a restraining order. We'll tell them that she left a concerning message, and for the safety of all of us we need to cut the cord."

I acquiesced with a nod but wondered if Sadie believed that I was all in now. I was all in, I really was, but I still wanted to have her number in my phone for ... whatever. When I went to the bathroom, I added Lily's number into my phone under a different name with the same ringtone.

Another hour passed and I collected my things to head home to Wes.

"I love you, Sadie. Just ... I love you," I said, still feeling a bit sheepish. "Elle, do you want to give G-Sep a hug and lock the door after me?"

"I'll follow you out," Sadie said, but as she tried to stand up, she doubled over and fell back down onto the sofa.

"My God, Sadie. What's wrong?"

"Whoosh!" she blurted. "Oh, boy, I just cramped up. Ooh."

"Okay, I'm not leaving here yet."

"Mommy, what's wrong?"

"Sep, just help me up from the sofa. I'll be fine, really."

I pushed the cocktail table away from the sofa and out-stretched my arms to help her up.

"Easy, Sadie. That's it."

Once she was in a standing position, I continued to support her in case she cramped up again.

"Look. Mommy peed!"

Sadie and I looked at each other before turning around, knowing the time had arrived.

"Don't worry, Elly. Your baby brother or sister is crying, and those are tears letting us know that he or she is ready to come out."

I must say that was a pretty clever explanation to give to a child!

"Is the baby coming out right now?" screeched Elle.

"Honey, G-Sep is going to call Daddy and he will come home. The doctor will want to see Mommy, and I'll stay here with you. Elly, please get a towel from the bathroom and put it on the seat of the kitchen chair. The baby has to dry its tears."

Once Sadie was seated, she called the doctor.

"Dr. Mead wants me to go straight to the hospital," she said when she ended the call. "Though I'm approximately two weeks away from my due date I was already dilated at my last visit."

I grabbed my phone.

"Hey, Josh. The eagle is about to land! Sadie called the obstetrics office and Dr. Mead, her obstetrician who delivered Elle, is on call."

Josh made it home in twenty minutes. Sadie changed her clothes, and her overnight bag was ready by the front door.

"Off we go!" Josh said and then picked up Elle.

"I want to go, too!" Elle protested.

"You're staying here with G-Sep and I'll call you as soon as the baby comes out."

"I'll call Wes and Jack and put them on alert," I said.

Sadie hugged both of us and was whisked away to bring another beautiful human into the world!

Wes arrived shortly thereafter and the three of us waited for the phone call. It wasn't until almost four hours later that Josh called in.

"Mommy and baby are doing well! Dr. Mead gave her a Pitocin drip to move things along and, once again, she delivered naturally."

"So, so … I have you on speaker now. Elle, especially, wants to know about her sibling."

"What does she want to know?" Josh laughed.

"Daddy, what is it?"

"Well, pumpkin, G-Sep and Grandpa will have to bring you

to the hospital to meet Cece."

"Cece! Cece! I have a baby sister! The magic wand really worked!"

"Let me go back inside to the delivery room now, but all of you are welcome to come to the hospital. Please call Jack and Adam. I'm sure that Adam will want to hear the news as well."

Elle and I packed a few of her toys, including a present that she picked out for the baby. I grabbed one of the small gifts that Sadie and I purchased for Elle. With all the excitement of a new baby, we wanted to be sure that Elle felt special.

Cecilia, seven pounds and two ounces, started to command everyone's attention the moment she arrived home! Elle fussed every morning about going to school, which was understandable. She wanted to feel secure that she maintained her attachment to Sadie now that there was a baby sister in the house. Jack had graciously allowed me to drop her off at his veterinary office a few afternoons a week to play with the dogs, a delightful distraction that afforded Sadie the time to develop a routine with Cece.

CHAPTER 29

Every Garden Grows Differently

I was relishing Cecilia's arrival, free of heart and mind, recognizing that if Lily were still attached to the fringes of our family blanket there would be underlying tension. Sadness for Lily still touched me, though, and I was reminded that she lost her baby. Her world pulled away from her in the wake of her madness, and now her roots in our family garden have been ripped from the rich earth so the other seeds can grow. Now more than ever I thought about the past and how differently we all journeyed. All of us had a story.

"Wes, you and I have been together for years and it is amazing how things pop into my head about the past. Out of nowhere, things that I've never shared with you."

"Oh, is that so?"

"Nothing shocking," I laughed, "but mostly about my insecurities growing up."

"Something specific that you want to share with me?"

"Just thinking about names and how untraditional my name is."

"It certainly is, but it's beautiful. I'll admit, I get a huge kick when I tell people your name. It raises eyebrows with a smile! You never told me how your parents came up with the name September."

"September Sarah Webb. Well, my mother, wanting to be nontraditional, learned of the name from a character in a movie. I suppose the name stuck in her head and then she coerced my father. They appeased the elders by giving me the name Sara as a middle name. I had a great aunt Sara, and Sara is also a biblical name."

"I never knew that."

"My great-grandfather emigrated here from Russia and shortened his last name from Weberberg to Webb. It was tough, back then, for a Jew to gain employment. I've always loved our last name because it didn't refer to a particular ethnicity. Growing up in Brooklyn I didn't have a large Jewish peer group and therefore was not socially supported by any strong Jewish influence. Names like Fogelberg and Feldman were the butt of ethnic jokes. The name Webb, however, granted me immunity from stereotypical comments and deflected any negative attention where my name is concerned. I'd chuckle along with the others, though, seeking their acceptance but at the same time feeling a sense of betrayal to my family and myself."

"Go on."

"September, however, is an eccentric first name. I had grown accustomed to being called 'flavor of the month.' I was a twelve-year-old girl by all standards, but the name September sounds 'risqué,' like a porn star's name, so I've been told.

Always shy and reserved, physically awkward, and cast aside by the boys, my self-esteem was in the toilet."

"I never would have known that, Sep. You're the epitome of confidence."

"My girlfriends, my besties, were assertive, physically blossoming, and earning the boys' attention. Wes, I would often stand naked in front of the bathroom mirror and stare at my non-existent breasts attached to a body skinny as a rail. Adding insult to injury, the shiny metal braces on my teeth that kept me company for two years made me even less appealing to the boys in the park. However, riding on the coattails of my trio of attractive girlfriends allowed me to feel important and connected, but I never felt comfortable in my own skin. Uh, I have no idea why I'm telling you all of this."

"Were your parents aware of how you were feeling?"

"Not at all. That was the part of me that I never wanted to share. They kept me on a pedestal, instilling in me that I could conquer the world! Though I was raised in a home with an overabundance of positivity and encouragement, when I stepped out of our apartment, I faced a very different reality."

"Go on, I'm learning a lot."

"Well, I think you know that my dad was an expert tailor?"

"Uh, yes, I do know that."

"My dad learned that skill when he was eighteen years old. He worked seven days a week in a small shop while Mom nurtured a loving home. We were strapped financially, but I felt like I had everything! In our small, one-bedroom apartment I slept in my twin bed, in the foyer with a blanket covering the entry to the living room so the light from the television wouldn't wake me at night. We lived in a castle. Wealth is more a feeling than something tangible. We were rich with simplicities, and Dad was king. No man could be held to a higher order."

"So, there is a reason why this is coming out, a reason why you want to talk about this. Correct?"

"I ... I was just thinking about one of our Valentine's Days."

"Okay."

I stayed silent.

"Okay," Wes said again.

"It was the wristlet, the corsage with the carnations. I was thinking about that, Wes."

"And?"

Tears started to accumulate in the buckets under my eyes. I looked away.

Wes placed two fingers under my chin and craned my head in his direction. Connecting his eyes with mine he said, "Tell me about the corsage."

"It touched me at my core. Please don't take this the wrong way."

"Honey, what would I take the wrong way?"

"Because in the past I was lavished with expensive things from worthless men. Beautiful, boxed roses that when I removed the long stems, I still felt as empty as the discarded cardboard box."

"And ...?"

"And when I peeked into the refrigerator and saw a simple wristlet from a man who is priceless, it was like an entire flower shop was bought for me. Jeez, you must think I'm nuts!"

Wes stared at me with kind eyes and said nothing.

"Wes, you are priceless. You are home to me. You hold us to what's important in life. With you, I feel like I'm with my dad ... but not like that! Not like I need a daddy figure." I giggled through my tears.

"You mean to say, I get you? Is that what you're trying to tell me?"

"Yes, you really do."

"Seppie, I've had a difficult upbringing and was the product of very poor parents. My dad passed away when I was seven and there was no money. When my grandparents passed on, they left us their house, and although it was paid off it was in desperate need of repair."

"Yes, you told me that."

"My momma tooled around town in an old brown Chevy station wagon and would frequently drive us to the Goodwill Clothing Drop. Sometimes excess donations were left outside the bin, and we'd load the bags into the trunk. Once we reached home, we were always surprised by what we would find. If there were children's clothes or other items that we couldn't use, we returned them to the bin."

"Oh, Wes," I said with sadness.

"What you don't know is that by the end of the week our refrigerator was bare. Potatoes and onion sandwiches were staples. Momma made some money by allowing neighborhood men to gamble in the privacy of our damp basement. My brothers and I played our own game upstairs, pulling straws to see who got the piece of bread with the mold. It really wasn't terrible because it was easy to scrape it off the bread. Food was never, ever thrown away or wasted. When I was old enough to work, I took a job at an ice cream shop after school, worked until closing, and my feet blistered from standing for so many hours. But I appreciated everything."

"I had no idea ..."

"Interesting, Seppie, that you and I should be having this

conversation, isn't it?"

"But the corsage, it …"

"Yes, let's get back to the corsage because it seems to have great significance."

"It's the pride thing, Wes. When you placed it on my wrist, I saw a light in your eyes that I used to see in my father's. Like … like when he would stop at this little store on the Lower East Side and bring home a small tin of Pastillines fruit drops or Sen-Sen licorice mint pieces in the foil packet. Little inexpensive candies that meant the world to me! Oh, it's just this feeling. Am I making sense?"

Wes listened intently, then responded, making the connection, "We hold separate pasts but have common threads."

"True, Wes, and you know that the relationships we have with our parents tells us something about how we will treat others."

"I certainly do. Interestingly, I never had money to buy Momma flowers. Mom loved carnations, and when I earned my first paycheck, I spent it in the flower shop. In retrospect, that Valentine's Day, I gave to you, the woman I love, what I gave to my first love, my momma."

And just like that, when I thought I couldn't get any closer to Wes … I could never be surer about becoming his wife.

"I am speechless, and breathless, and whatever," I said and kissed him gently. "I love where we came from. I love where we are."

"As do I."

I wandered around our apartment a bit aimlessly to straighten up, still focused on our conversation. I lifted a sweater from the chair, sat down, and held it to my cheek. Deep in thought, I mused about my daddy sitting at his sewing machine for hours with tired eyes stitching garments for other people. He'd sometimes take me to work, and I'd watch him organize the wooden spools of thread while I ate my sandwich.

He spun the fabric of our family.

CHAPTER 30

The Scrapbook

Summer had just begun, and steam was rising from the sidewalks. A sweltering-hot day for the end of June. Today was the last day on Adam's lease, and while he was en route to Wisconsin, I arrived at his apartment early that morning with my Starbucks and Little Playmate cooler to oversee the move. I volunteered to bag any random items left behind as well as broom-clean the rooms.

The moving truck finally pulled up over two hours after my arrival. I sat on the small kitchen step stool and watched them cart away pieces of Lily's life. Baby T's crib was disassembled and brought to the side of the building for Lily's retrieval. The restraining order didn't permit her to be within a certain number of feet of the premises, but Adam spoke with the building superintendent and agreed to leave it for her. Two large boxes, labeled "Baby T's Toys" and "Baby T's Clothes," would be left alongside the crib.

My senses deadened as my mind drifted to the day I had moved into Teddy and Lily's house. Sweet, vulnerable, Lily, whom I had tried to mold into the kind of girl that Sadie was, giving her the same tools to blossom into a wholesome woman. Was it nature or nurture? I had nurtured Lily, but she had Teddy's nature, cut from his soiled cloth and a product of his influence.

The movers were carrying the last few boxes down the stairs and I followed behind them. Once loaded onto the truck, they slammed the back door shut and latched it. I signed the necessary paperwork on their clipboard, then handed each mover a generous tip. And, mesmerized, I stood in front of the brownstone watching the truck pull away from the curb, hauling the remnants of a broken marriage and the end of a chapter. It made me wonder if movers were ever curious about the back stories of the items they were transporting, if they wondered whether someone's storyline would end at the end of that day job or whether the tenants were traveling from one destination to another due to unforeseen circumstances. Each dish, each piece of furniture, had a history of its own.

Sluggishly I walked to the front of the building to begin my trek up the three long flights of stairs. It felt like a lifetime since I first visited Lily in this apartment. Brownie, her dog, had since perished, but the doormat, *Every Day is Hump Day,* still greeted guests. I rolled it up and added it to the heavy trash bag in the apartment. The heels of my shoes created an echo as I walked from room to room, taking inventory of what I would no longer come back to: the familiarity of two wonderful people who added dimension to my family. The same emptiness had consumed me when I was summoned to leave Teddy's house.

Dragging the trash bag behind me, I added to it a toilet bowl brush but left the half-filled can of Ajax under the bathroom sink. The corner of the bedroom floor had one dusty, satin hair scrunchy waiting for pickup, and in the closet, an empty plastic suit bag. On the living room windowsill three dead plants commemorated this gloomy day. Dead plants, apropos for the occasion. I tossed them.

Bzzzzz, bzzzz.

"Hey, Wes. Yes. Yes, the movers have come and gone. Yeah, I'm just cleaning up. I'll call you shortly. Okay, okay, see you soon."

I put the phone down next to my cooler on the kitchen counter and began checking for items that needed to be trashed. Two sets of chopsticks and a cocktail fork in the drawer, some mismatched plastic containers and lids, and one of the vintage drinking glasses. I stepped up onto the stool to check the top cabinets and had déjà vu. I hadn't thought about the top cabinet above the sink since the day I was here stocking their refrigerator before their return from their honeymoon.

The cabinet to the right of the recipe books housed a large serving platter received as a wedding gift. When I opened the cabinet with the books, a Mason jar was still balanced on top of the recipe books and the album. My anxiety eased. Everything looked intact and maybe, just maybe, the two disturbing entries that I once discovered were random incidents, lending themselves to Lily's adjustment to our family.

Once the platter and Mason jar were brought down to the counter, I balanced the books in my hands and stepped down from the stool. Amazing that Lily never moved out with her beautiful collection of recipe books and Adam didn't check the top cabinets. Holding the books, I gently kicked the step stool into the living room and positioned it against a wall. Sitting with the books between my legs, I pulled the album from the pile. Resting it on my knees and taking a deep breath, I was cognizant of why I had never mentioned this to Sadie, Wes, or Adam. I always loved Lily so deeply and never wanted to expose her flaws, nor did I ever want to expose Teddy's.

The album felt a bit bulkier than what I remembered, and I opened the jacket to uncover the first page. It was the clipping I had seen before from Sadie and Josh's wedding from the Sunday edition of *The New York Times* in which, in red ink, Sadie's and Josh's names had been crossed out and Lily's and Adam's had replaced them. On the following page, the two pictures of Elle were present, and written above it, "Our Precious Baby Elle" with the clipping of her hair in a Ziploc. That wasn't all ....

Every page that followed bore deep jealousies of Sadie as well as her disappointment in me, insinuating that I was a weak woman who should have abandoned her father before he "gave me the ax." The red markings and comments were intimidating and crushing and made me feel like the butt of a Marlboro tossed on the sidewalk, then squashed with the sole of her shoe.

Page five. Lily and Adam's wedding. A photo of Sadie in her '60s dress with a crushed sunflower taped to the page. Heading: "You tried to steal the show with your fucking hippie braids. Always your one-upmanship! Why didn't you go braless, too, bitch?"

Page six. A photo of Elle at their wedding wearing our family's tiara, and taped to the page, five rhinestones. Heading: "Smelly Elly, that should have been *mine* to wear! Whoever wears it next will certainly not shine!"

Page seven: Smeared, dried, pink and blue frosting decorated the paper. Heading: "Your announcement about baby number two ruined my party! Guess one could say that you 'robbed the cradle'? It would have been fun to shove these cupcakes up Sadie's ass and crush one in Elly's face! Hahahahaha!"

Lily's comments were puerile and frightening. The shaking of my hands and the sick feeling in the pit of my stomach had taken over.

Page eight: The glossy picture of Baby T's sonogram occupied this page. A thin, red felt marker added arms and legs extending from this tiny picture of a developing baby. Heading: "The world *unwelcomes* you."

With the turn of each page I suffered in silence, experiencing the stages of grief like a clusterfuck. If there were a hole in my chest, I would have bled out from my heart.

Shock, disbelief, and anger all battled for my attention but in the end, there would be no more bargaining and no more denial, only acceptance. In the beginning my connection to Lily had allowed me to hold onto a fragment of Teddy, but then it truly became all about Lily. She was a microcosm of her father, no fault of her own, and had that special magic, which had torn my heart out.

No, September, we won't use that as a bargaining chip, will we?

Both were fragmented, broken, cunning, and carried the demon seed. Heat rose to my face as I read each entry, holding tightly to my good emotional health with a reminder that I couldn't control another's shortcomings. I could not allow Lily's demolition to shatter me, to pull me down into the dungeon of her private hell.

Out there on the sea those distress flares from distant ships were bright, a warning to turn my vessel around, yet I was drawn to the light. Juxtaposed, I supposed? It was only then that I could see things clearly, that opening my heart and widening my eyes to search for the good in Teddy and Lily had blinded me.

Adam would never know how much he had been saved. Stillborn Baby T would be born again, would resurface into a better life than what she would have had with Lily. If Lily had been able to work through her demons, I believed she could have been a good mother. It was only then, in that apartment, in that moment, that I was free.

The numbing in my body made it difficult to stand, but I rose to my feet and tossed the recipe books into the trash bag, tying a knot at the top. I exited the apartment and pulled the trash bag down the flights of stairs, the album and the platter under my arm. Once outside the brownstone, the sanitation truck in front began emptying the trash cans.

"Ma'am, I'll take that from you."

"Oh, thank you!"

"What about what you're holding?"

I handed him the platter.

"Is that it?"

"Yes, that's all," I said as I held the album in both hands. "I'll dispose of this."

"Have a lovely day, miss."

"You as well."

I turned away and walked to the side of the building where the crib and two boxes were awaiting Lily's pickup. As I tried to wedge the album between two slats in the crib, I sensed someone behind me, perhaps the sanitation worker, and turned around.

Lily.

She stood in front of me and said nothing. I wanted to hug her tightly and cry with her. Cry tears of happiness for all the years we'd been together. And forgive her and forgive me and, oh, just everything. But when I searched her eyes, I couldn't find a connection.

"Lily."

Nothing.

"Can I hug you, Lily?"

Despondency.

I removed the album from the slats in the crib and held it out at arm's length in front of me. "Why?"

The emptiness in her eyes became fiery, and her face distorted. Frightening. I became worried.

"Lily, please let us help you. We know you aren't the person you've been displaying and you're not responsible for the sad things that have happened in your life. We can find the right support to bring back our Lily. We'll all do this together."

"You can go fuck yourself, Seppie. I don't want or need your help."

"But I want to—"

"I could care less about what *you* want or think. You know what? Our time has come and gone."

She walked over to the crib and kicked it hard with the heel of her shoe, breaking one of the slats. "I don't want that crib or any of the crap in those boxes. Tell Adam he can shove it up his ass."

"Oh, please, Lily, let's—"

"Get the fuck away from me, you imposter! Never mention my name. And if God is truly good to me, we'll never see each other again."

I went silent, feeling scared and out of my element.

Then she relaxed and showed a twisted smile. "Seppie, the album is your keepsake. A gift from me to you."

She turned her head to the side, spat on the ground, and then walked away from me. I watched her until she was no longer in my view. I watched her walk out of my life forever.

The small flower garden in front was already blooming, and I took it upon myself to pull a few tulips. Purple tulips. Significant.

Once upstairs, I filled the Mason jar with water, arranged the flowers, and placed the jar on the windowsill.

"Hi, Wes. I'll meet you in front. All done here. Will just grab my cooler and lock up. Yes. Will see you in a bit."

I crossed the threshold and looked back into the empty apartment.

The tulips were lovely on the windowsill but would wither away, along with every good memory.

CHAPTER 31

The Call

My family garden sprouted all good things with the change of the seasons. Chilly days didn't seem so harsh; I arrived at a peaceful place in my life that served as a warm blanket. Wes and I kept a busy schedule with travel plans and stepping in as a second set of parents to our grandchildren when needed. Jack informed us that he and Callie, his veterinary anesthetist who he had partnered with, were in a serious relationship.

The spring and summer months had always been my favorites but when September rolls in, Wes and I will be united as husband and wife. All around, love is in the air!

This morning, I woke up earlier than Wes and grabbed the opportunity to sit on our terrace, taking in the quiet of New York City before it opens its eyes.

"Seppie, let's do something different today," Wes announced as he poked his head out on the terrace.

"Oh, what do you have in mind?"

"Something you wouldn't expect from me," he smiled. "Let's visit the Brooklyn Botanical Garden. It's not oppressively hot, which makes it easy to stroll around there for mid-August. No time like the present. If you go online there may be interesting exhibits. You'd know much better than I."

"That sounds like a plan, and very romantic. Regardless of the exhibits, let's do it! Honey, would you mind bringing my coffee out to the terrace and joining me?"

"Will do. Be right there."

More than ten minutes passed.

"Wes?"

No response.

"Wes, did you get lost in the kitchen?" I called out again, raising my voice in case he hadn't heard me.

No response.

"I have a sneaking suspicion that my coffee did not come out the way I like it. Is that true? Wes?"

I lifted myself off the cushioned patio chair and pulled the sliding glass door fully open.

"Wes, now I'm coming to get you *and* my coffee! This better not be a trick to get me back into the apartment to find you naked in our bed, or something," I laughed.

"Wes?"

Wes was not in the kitchen, but sure enough, when I peeked into the bedroom, he was sitting at the edge of our bed by his nightstand, talking quietly. I stood silent by the door.

"What on earth are you ...?"

The phone was pressed tightly to his ear and when I entered the room he cupped his other ear with his hand, as if I was interrupting his conversation. I continued to stand there quietly, thinking it strange that he would take a conversation into another room.

Wes then turned around to look at me with a solemn gaze, and I observed that he was visibly upset.

"Wes?" I whispered, trying to get his attention.

"I see," he said to the person on the other end. "Yes, yes. Obviously, you did the right thing by telling me and I will pass this on to the others. For sure. Are you okay? Okay. Will you be coming here at all ...? Because you always have a place to stay. Very well. Take care."

When Wes disconnected from the call, I stood in front of him with a puzzled look. He said nothing.

"Who was that?"

Wes looked at me, sallow, the color from his face drained.

"Wes?"

"Um. Oh, Seppie. Oh, dear."

Wes was struggling with something. My body was numb. *Please, God, let my family be okay!*

"Wes, who was that?"

"It was Adam."

"Adam? We haven't heard from him in a while. Is he all right? Is his mother not well?"

"They are fine. Can we sit down?"

"You're scaring me," I said, tensing up, my hands shaking uncontrollably. Wes grabbed them in his.

"No, no, no! No, Wes, no!" I whimpered, but in my head, I was screaming.

Wes pulled me in, pulling me tight up against him until I could barely breathe, then released me.

"There was an accident. Some ..."

I know, I know, I know.

My hands were pushing tightly on my ears because I didn't

want to hear anymore.

"I'm so sorry, love. Lily is gone."

I looked at Wes with confusion.

"Gone? Gone where?"

Wes looked down.

"She's not gone!" I yelled at him.

Wes looked up and our eyes locked.

"She can't be gone," I giggled. "Even though we haven't heard from her she's started anew somewhere else, living her life the way she should with all the good things we gave her. Because she will always be our Lily, regardless."

"I'm so sorry, Sep."

I continued to laugh, and Wes' expression didn't change. I laughed hysterically.

"Why do you say such things? Why? Why, why, why?!"

I pounded my fists hard on his chest until my frenzied giggles became tears. Buckets of tears to cry me a river.

Lily, bouncing between her struggles and twinkles of hope for brighter tomorrows, was gone. Just gone. Wes informed the family, and our apartment was quiet, allowing me the space to absorb her tragedy, my tragedy, too. No details of the accident were given to us, which I was certain would surface later, but at that moment, I needed quiet. There had not been proper closure. Both she and Teddy had died, and both would never know how much of myself I had given away. That day when Lily walked away from me, she left me physically, but she still lived within me. That very tragic day that I hadn't been able to talk about.

No specifics about burial arrangements were shared with Wes, nor did Adam inquire if we had contributing thoughts. I was not comfortable interceding about next steps and supposed it was Adam's decision regarding how to proceed, being the closest of kin, the only person who had been contacted.

Three days later Adam reached out again to Wes to inform us that the burial arrangements had been made. There were no details about his travel plans to New York to wrap up the remains of her short life. Had he considered a funeral service with a proper send-off? I had no answers, but I did have questions and had hoped there could have been collaboration.

Finally, Adam called me.

"Hi, Seppie. I waited to reach out to you. This has been a nightmare, for you, too, I can only imagine. I'm never at a loss for words but this, well, I struggled to …"

"Yes. Yes, Adam," I answered with flat affect.

"Please understand that …"

"Adam, I do understand. Lily was like a daughter, a part of me, although she caused so much heartache. Right or wrong, I continued to enforce damage control so everyone could see her in the best light, even though there were signs that concerned me. There's so much that you may not have known …"

"Seppie, she and I struggled from the very beginning, and I surmised that her erratic behavior was a manifestation of childhood trauma. Remember, we met in a bereavement group when her father was dying from Alzheimer's, and though she never shared specifics, I do know that her mother died from terminal illness. That is a heavy load to lug around. I chose to stay. Perhaps wishful thinking on my part that the strength of our love for her, and your solid family behind us, would help us to ride out the storm. This is not your burden to carry."

"Adam," I said through my tears, "the last time I saw her was when I was cleaning out your apartment. She showed up outside the building where you left the crib and boxes, and

I was startled. She said terrible things to me, but even so, I encouraged her to allow us to find her some professional support. It was to no avail. But that support could have saved her.”

“Only if someone wants to be saved, and you know that. She did love all of us, Seppie, with whatever she had in her toolbox. You know, as well as I, that it’s difficult to change a person’s trajectory.”

I swallowed hard, holding back tears, and remained silent.

“Are you still with me?”

“Yes, Adam.”

“Lily is buried next to her parents, just so you know. Block 77, row 7, grave 7. I loved Lily with all my heart, Seppie. Don’t ever think for a moment that my intention was to cold-heartedly bury her.”

“But no service? All of us are her family. Adam, I must know how Lily …”

“I did my best under the circumstances and her untimely death came as a hard blow. The conditions surrounding her death will scar you as it has scarred me. Please, please trust me. I was informed that Lily was unrecognizable after the accident, and I couldn’t ask you to try to identify her body. Seppie, do you understand?”

I could hear his struggle. Internally I was broken and falling apart. I was suffocating. There were no words.

“Seppie, my thought is to plan a small memorial with just the family, perhaps in a place that was special to her. I will fly back to New York in a few weeks and that should give us time to absorb this tragedy and think more clearly.”

“Yes, that would be lovely for her,” I responded robotically with a hoarseness in my voice. I had to know how my Lily died, but at the moment, could I push him beyond his limit when he was suffering, too?

"I'm so sorry, but I need to end our call now," Adam said. "You're in my thoughts. Always. I will reach out to you again."

"Adam?"

"Yes."

"How did she die?"

Silence.

"Adam. How did Lily die?"

My heart was pounding out of my chest, waiting for his answer. An impending storm was approaching, and I felt I would drown once the rain made its descent.

"Adam."

"Oh, Seppie. Lily drove a car off a cliff at Devil's Leap. A preserve in Connecticut closed for restoration. Lily was decapitated."

I heard a deep inhale, then he disconnected, and the phone call went dead. The airwaves swept away my imaginary lifeline to Lily. Adam had wanted to do the right thing for all of us, but he was gone, and it would be unfair to keep him bound to a family that no longer existed.

Making Peace, in Peace

All of us were a product of our experiences. Lily wasn't on solid ground; she was a broken girl, a crack in the porcelain. I can only take responsibility for my actions. Not being a part of her solution, in an indirect way, made me a part of the problem. I chose to look away. She was right. Shame on me!

Important life events could stimulate a person's trauma if transition periods were difficult. Her casualties of losing both parents, getting married without her parents, losing a baby, and then her marriage, combined with having a surrogate family, qualified for the grand prize of creating an overloaded circuit breaker. I didn't know the circumstances surrounding Lily's death, nor did Adam know the circumstances surrounding her mother's death.

I never shared the contents of her mother's letter with anyone and honored her wishes to keep it our secret. Lily wanted her mother's death to have some dignity, and I granted her that latitude, even now in her death. Her mother was black-mailed. The emotional turmoil of powerlessness that she had felt must have been analogous to being trapped in a burning building with no escape. Conceivably, Adam was allowing Lily to have some dignity? That poignant moment gave me a sneak preview into why people went fucking mad, batshit crazy, or toyed with the concept of self-harm.

I imagined Lily standing rigid on a precipice, believing that there was no one who would pull her back.

After an hour and five minutes I reached the exit, followed the signs, and drove through the gates. The guard standing inside the entrance motioned me to roll down my window and I handed him the notecard with the address.

"Very good, ma'am. It's not too far from here. Just follow this road straight up, turn right at the end, and it will be clearly marked."

Following his close instructions, I reached my destination and pulled over, close to the small curb that divided the grass from the road. Few visitors had their cars parked nearby, the beautiful weather encouraging loved ones to bring fresh flowers.

I reached for my tote on the passenger seat and became fixated on the index card with the cemetery information. This was the first time that the number 7 had struck a chord. That number had been popping up everywhere, eerily sending me some message, like it was a warning sign. Once out of the car I padded to the location, respectful of where I was stepping. An instant chill in the air, with a slight wind gust, blanketed the warmth of this Indian summer fall day.

The Gods are with me, giving me a signal. You've got this, Sep.

As I approached the graves, two with their headstones side-by-side, it was unsettling to see Lily's freshly dug ditch, filled in with dirt, to the right of her mother's. The graves surrounding the Zezza plot were beautifully manicured, evidence that loved ones visited and invested in the upkeep. No fresh flowers sat on Teddy's and Tessa's grave, next to Lily's soft mound of dark fresh dirt, and the weeds had not been pulled from around her parents' headstones. I didn't recall Lily or Adam mentioning that they visited here to pay respects.

Others must have walked by the Zezza plot, gawking at it like it was the shittiest house on the block. There wasn't a better way to describe it. Unequivocally, as time passed, weeds would grow wild around Lily's grave because it had ended a chapter for my family, and me, who truly loved her. Her last page in our story book.

Kneeling down next to the mound, I dug my hand into my small fabric tote. In it, I removed a bunch of purple tulips that I bought from our corner market and laid them across the middle of the mound, positioning them where her heart might be, deep down beneath the earth. Wrapped thick in tissue paper, I removed the next item and uncovered the tiara that I had purchased for her on the Valentine's Day when I was attacked. Lily vehemently sought after my family's heirloom and I wanted her to have one of her own to give to her daughter, to start her own tradition. I placed it where I envisioncd her head would be.

"Go to the angels, like the princess you always wanted to be. A pity that you thought you had to work so hard for it. You were always a princess to me."

My phone sat on the ground to the right of me, and I stared at it before picking it up. I deleted Lily's contact under the fictitious name I created, "NN" for "No Name." Sadness consumed me, reflecting on the range of emotions I experienced over the years whenever I had heard the gaggle of geese. Spanning from childhood to adulthood, Lily's inner conflict dictated the tenor of our relationship.

I stood up, brushed the dirt from the knees of my jeans, and walked over to Teddy's and Tessa's graves, pitifully sad. Grabbing the weeds in my fists I began pulling them out from around their headstones. Ripping and pulling with fierce determination, sweat dripping from my brow, I tossed the weeds to the side until her parents' names were exposed on the slate. Lily would want her final resting place to be with whom she had her roots.

Close to half an hour later I created an ugly artform of two dried-out weed piles, then stood in front of the three plots. Gently separating a tulip from the bunch on Lily's grave, I placed it on her mother's, then returned to Lily's.

"This is your garden."

CHAPTER 33

September in September

"To everything, turn, turn, turn. There is a season, turn, turn, turn. And a time to every purpose, la, la, la, la … Ah, Central Park is simply beautiful this time of year, Sadie. The perfect month to get married," I said.

"September in September! Well, you're up early?"

"I hardly slept a wink," I said, exiting the bathroom with a towel wrapped around me.

"Are you nervous, soon-to-be Mrs. Harlow?"

"Nervous? Nah. Should I be?" I laughed. "I'm feeling excited … and grateful that you and Elle stayed overnight. I hope that Josh and Wes are good with the baby."

"They are. Our sitter is coming over to help with Cece today because Wes will need Josh's assistance getting ready. Remember, Wes is the other half in this celebration, right?"

"He sure is!"

"Danye will be here at 8:30, with her cosmetician, and once

us girls are dolled up, Elly and I will cab it back to my place to
get dressed."

"Sadie, thank you. Thank you for ..."

"We've spent nearly the entire night talking. There is absolutely *nothing* that I wouldn't do for you. Trust me, this wedding will prove to be everything you can imagine. We left no
stone unturned. Do you trust me?"

"I do, I do."

"Girl, save the 'I do's' for later!"

We laughed.

I dried the wetness from my hair and thought that Elle was
still sleeping until I heard her call out.

"G-Sep, the downstairs is buzzing!"

"I'll get it, Sep." Sadie hustled to the door.

A few minutes later the front door opened and closed.

"Oh, boy! Look at this box, G-Sep!" Elle announced this so
loudly that I'm certain my neighbors heard her!

"Way too early for this delivery," Sadie puffed.

"Why? What is it?"

"It's the flowers. Before I make room for them in the refrigerator, I'm just going to check the order. Okay? Okay ... I see
yours, but where is Wes' boutonniere? Um ... yes, it's here."
Sadie looked up. "But, Sep?"

"Yes."

"We have to call the florist."

"Really, why?"

"I don't think they sent the correct flowers."

After putting on my robe, I strolled to the kitchen to check
the delivery. The flowers were the only thing Sadie allowed me
to control. She and Wes did it all.

"Oh, my, they're perfect! There's a reason why I decided on

these flowers. Come have a look, Elle," I called.

The smile on my face was ear to ear, and Sadie looked at both Elle and me strangely.

"They're so pretty, G-Sep!" Elle yelled.

"Yes, they are."

"They're very pretty," Sadie agreed. "Different. Not quite the traditional wedding bouquet, but I do love it."

Adam had called yesterday to congratulate Wes and me and offer heartfelt good wishes. He sounded content and settled, living back in Wisconsin. Though he respectfully declined the invitation to our wedding he would always be regarded as family, but I sensed that he was gently detaching. His life in New York had ended unpredictably and traumatically.

At 8:15 Danye arrived and began setting up at the dining room table. Seeing her again gave me a hauntingly familiar déjà vu, causing me to think back to Lily's wedding, but she didn't ask about her. Both artists worked efficiently within the time frame to style our hair and apply our makeup. A touch of blush and lip gloss brightened Elle's small face.

"Elle, honey, before you and Mommy leave, I have something for you. Come here."

"I know what it is," she sang. "Nah, nah, nah, nah, nah."

"Oh, you do?"

The velvet pouch held our family heirloom, with the re-attached rhinestones that I had scraped off Lily's scrapbook page. A local craft shop had worked wonders; one would never know they had been missing.

While Danye secured the tiara on Elle's head, Sadie escorted me into the bedroom to help me slip into my dress.

"Gorg ... Sep. Gorg!" yelled Sadie. "Finish dressing and I'll follow Danye out. Elly and I need to get home to change. We'll see you there. Give me a hug."

Once the front door closed, I sat at the end of the bed and took a deep breath, giving myself a few minutes to take inventory of my life after having my fair share of personal challenges. Reevaluating the past, appreciating the gift of today, and internalizing that I was deserving of a fulfilling future pushed away the obstacles that had pulled me off my path to self-appreciation.

I then walked over to the bathroom mirror, stared at myself for a good, long time, and planted a kiss on it, leaving a lipstick mark. *Seppie, I love you!*

Jack burst into my apartment. "Your coach has arrived!"

My son had the distinct honor of escorting me to Central Park. The front door was unlocked, and Jack let himself in while Callie waited in the car service. I knew that the others would already be there so I could make a grand entrance without Wes ogling me ahead of time.

"Damn! A damn cougar is what you are! Mama, look at you!"

I blushed.

"Really, Jack? First off, Wes is older than I, and secondly, I'm over the age limit to be called a cougar. I might be in the bison category! Okay … grab the flowers from the refrigerator and away we go!"

"Mom, you're no bison!"

I stepped into my heels with the pearls around the ankle strap.

"Okay, Jack … I'm doin' it. Time to go."

Once downstairs, Jack opened the back door of the car for me and I greeted Callie, and … another girl?

"Mom. Meet Lola," Jack introduced.

"You're bringing two girls to the wedding, Jack?"

"And Callie found the perfect outfit for Lola to wear to your wedding!"

I slithered into the seat next to Callie and held her hand.

"I'm so glad that you're part of this wedding day, Cal." Then I whispered to her, "Lola?"

Jack moved in next to me and had Lola sit on his lap. During the ride she and I exchanged peculiar looks, and I was concerned about everyone's reaction upon our arrival.

The car cruised down the avenues and wedding jitters began to settle in. We were dropped off at West 72nd and Central Park West, and then Jack put us in a pedicab that brought us close to the location of the ceremony, their best kept secret from me. Part of their wedding planning was to surprise me with the exact location to exchange our vows.

After a short distance, the pedicab dropped us off where we could see Bow Bridge, an iconic landmark. Many proposals had taken place at that spot; it had a reputation. Jack walked with Callie and Lola on each side of him and I followed close behind.

Just for a moment, I stopped to look up. A cool, inviting breeze met me. The sky, a bit overcast, was a good omen that no one would be raining on my parade.

CHAPTER 34

Our Storybook

My family came into view when we approached one of the landings beneath the bridge, and a range of emotions strongarmed my composure. A canopy of ivory tulle adorned this rustic landing, along with two wooden benches lined with lace cushions for our dearest observers. The perfect marriage of elegance and nature, with Bow Bridge as its backdrop.

Party Panache on the Park created our long-awaited, perfect Manhattan wedding. Sadie and Wes understood the emotional strain that I endured, this past year, and they worked as a team to keep the stress of wedding planning off my plate. With great appreciation, I trusted them to take the reins.

Elle ran toward us and straight to Lola, giggling when she saw the dog dressed in pink booties and a huge bow around her neck. Elle looked a little confused, until Sadie and Josh formally introduced them.

"Elly, this is Lola. She is yours! Take the leash from Uncle

Jack."

Lola barked and Elle cried, "She's mine? She's really mine?"

"You've been such a good girl helping us celebrate at Mommy's baby sprinkle and welcoming Baby Cece, and now at G-Sep's wedding. So, Daddy and I asked Uncle Jack to find the perfect puppy for you. We know how much you love King Charles Spaniels and know you'll love Lola!"

Elle knelt and hugged the life out of the small pooch until she squealed, then growled, then urinated on Elle's shoe. Oh, well.

"Elle," laughed Jack. "I'll teach you how to take care of her, okay?"

Elle kicked off her shoes and decided to go barefoot. *Today, I figured, anything goes!*

Wes stood by the canopy, hands clasped in front of him. He watched me approach him wearing a simple, ankle-length fitted silk taupe dress with a pearl choker. His smile was killer, and I wanted to pinch myself to make sure that this moment was real.

"Mom, where should I put the box?"

"Jack, honey, can you hold it while I take out the flowers?"

I removed the white carnation boutonniere from the small plastic box.

"A carnation?" Wes had a look of surprise!

I fastened it to the lapel on Wes' linen suit jacket with the large straight pin.

"But of course? Your mother needs to have presence here, today."

He began to tear up.

"Wes. Please help me with my flowers?" I asked as I lifted them out of the box.

I handed him a corsage the length of my entire forearm, filled with white carnations, with three bands to hold it on my arm. His expression? Priceless!

"What did you do?" he asked.

"This is my forever flower. Please slide it onto my arm."

The violinist, seated close to the canopy, began playing "Somewhere Over the Rainbow" while our family seated themselves on the bench. Next to Cece, asleep in her carriage, Elle laid out one of the baby's blankets to curl up with Lola on the ground.

And as if he'd known us forever, the officiant introduced us by eloquently reciting our memories that eventually defined us as a couple. Wesley Harlow looked more striking than ever, deep in thought absorbing each recollection. I watched the wind disturb his hair, and it blew me away, becoming lost in my love for him.

I was certain that Wes was the elusive image who floated in and out of my dreams, whom I'd searched for. In my dreams I could never catch him, awakening each time he was in my reach. But the universe placed him in my path when the stars aligned because the stars knew best when we were equipped to create something bigger than ourselves. The universe worked in mysterious ways.

Our family's abundance of love smothered us during our exchange of vows, then released itself to the skies over Bow Bridge, announcing to the world we were one. It was official!

The photographer whisked Wes and me up to the bridge, where she asked many a passerby to jump into our pictures, directing them to give their expressions each time we posed. So very New York City!

We picnicked on Cherry Hill on a blanket with an assortment of gourmet baguettini sandwiches, charcuterie, and fresh fruit, spilling from antique wicker picnic baskets. A petit fours and macaron tower from Magnolia Bakery completed the sweetness of a day that transcended to a long-overdue reunion.

Elle giggled, Lola howled softly, and Cece stirred. All music to my ears in our little cocoon. Amidst the symphony of the chatter my eyes became drawn to the picnic blanket.

No, not a picnic blanket. A quilt? An enormous quilt made from patches that told a story. Our story. Individual patches crafted by our loved ones and sewn together to ...

Oh, wow ... to breathe life into the fabric of our family.

Captivated by every square, the surrounding conversations became background.

I knew a tartan square cut from the blanket in the treehouse must be Wes', and the square with the peace sign had to be Sadie's. There were other squares that signified my grandchildren, and the edges of the masterpiece had little silver bobbins, no doubt my husband's idea.

And within the assembly of this cloth storybook, my eyes became hyper-focused on the patch with a purple tulip, added to our family's framework.

"You like?" Wes moved close to me.

"I love."

He stretched his legs out in front of him and leaned back on his elbows.

"Rest your head in my lap, Mrs. Harlow. Relax. We did it."

Billowy clouds bounced around above us, then a stream of sunlight pushed through to make its congratulatory entrance. It shone brightly, compelling my eyes to close until I was on the brink of sleep.

"Fresh flowers! Beautiful lilies! Ten dollars! Only ten dollars! Fresh flowers! Beautiful lilies! Ten dollars! Only ten dollars!"

In my dreamlike state, all I could hear was "Lily, Lily, Lily."

The voice carried loudly, drowning out the conversations around the quilt. Feeling drowsy, I struggled to open my eyes and raise my head off Wes' lap.

"Fresh flowers! Beautiful lilies! Ten dollars! Only ten dollars!"

A shabbily dressed old woman circled the area selling bunches of flowers from a large plastic bucket.

Lily. Lily. Poor Lily, I thought.

The woman moved closer to our blanket. "Fresh flowers! Beautiful lilies! Ten dollars! Only ten dollars!"

I looked at her bucket of lilies and she gazed at me, as if she could read me.

"You like some lilies? I give you two bunch of lilies for ten dollars. Yes? You want lilies?"

The chatter came to a halt and there was silence. All eyes were on me.

"Lilies?" I asked the woman. My eyes locked with hers, and she smiled.

Sadie stood up. "Yes, ma'am! We'd love some lilies!"

Wes pulled out his wallet. "How much for the bucket?"

Memories of you, dear child, my muse
Your face, a palette of lovely warm hues
An untouched canvas, open and bare
The stroke of my hand on your baby fine hair

Innocent eyes, your windows to pain
Followed my lead through darkness and rain
The highway of life is an uncertain ride
A balancing act, your arms only so wide

Perfect for you, perfect for you
I carried the weight of being perfect for you
So, you, my child, can be perfect for you

The things that tumble, sometimes shatter
And what you mend are the things that matter
Through triumph and tragedy, seeking to find
How to leave your footprints behind

Time escapes us, the years unfurl
Making your way in an imperfect world
Still searching my palette to finish your portrait
For others to value, love, and interpret

Perfect for you, perfect for you
I carried the weight of being perfect for you
So, you, my child, can be perfect for you

But it's the stroke of your brush, my beautiful pearl
That completes the story of a perfect girl

Who defines perfect?

First and foremost, I have to thank my parents for encouraging me, at a very young age, to dream big! My greatest teachers who taught from the heart, your lessons on patience, self-appreciation, and the importance of remaining grounded gave me wings to fly.

To my children, Samantha Rae and Dean Spencer, you are truly the greatest of my accomplishments and my character is best judged by how you have blossomed into strong, wise, and successful adults. I taught you integrity and kindness and now you are guiding that moral compass.

Samantha Rae, your artistic talent, budding since elementary school, has transcended to a career as an award-winning designer. It gives me insurmountable pride that you designed this book cover, and the book cover for *Searching for Septem-*

ber, to capture the true essence of both storylines. A picture is worth a thousand words!

To Scott, my younger brother and punching bag until you were old enough to strong-arm me, I love you to pieces! Though "partners in crime" since childhood, somehow, we created balance for each other. Our beautiful families have enriched our journey. So glad we decided to keep you!

My deep appreciation to Tony Ford, my dear friend and fellow writer, who has spent endless hours listening to my reading each chapter upon its completion. *Searching for September* and *Following the Fall* have been my labors of love, and your continual love and encouragement have helped me to deliver both babies!

A huge thank you to Maxine Berger, my friend, neighbor, and beta reader for the sequel. Having read both books, your attention to the details provided me with invaluable food for thought.

After quite a bit of digging I discovered my publisher, Cheryl Benton. Cheryl, you are truly the diamond in the rough! Your commitment to my characters, and finding value in my work as a writer, have brought their stories to life! As we eagerly continue to promote *Searching for September* and *Following the Fall* to a wide audience, readers are connected to the charm, challenges, and choices that surround relationships.

As women, it is crucial to acknowledge, and own, our feelings about our relationships. The role we play needs to be clear, and in partnership with discovering our voice. Shared experiences incentivized me to construct the characters in *Searching for September* and continue their journey in *Following the Fall*. I listened and heard, and our affirmations reverberate through the life of my characters.

ABOUT THE AUTHOR

Robin Lieberman, a native New Yorker born in Brooklyn, has remained true to her roots by raising her daughter and son in New York with its buzzing, unparalled energy. Ms. Lieberman resides in Manhattan and fills her personal life with world travel and quality time with her family and intimate circle of friends.

She began her career as a school counselor in her early twenties, serving students in the public school system for more than thirty-nine years. Their academic, social, and emotional needs continue to spark her passion to mold impressionable young adults as they struggle toward adulthood.

While fulfilling a career in education she has nurtured her writing through memoirs and poetry. Ms. Lieberman's triumphs through both personal disappointments and un-bounded joys have given her the impetus to share a view of the world through her lens, with creative and vivid imagination. *Following the Fall*, the sequel to *Searching for September*, invites her audience to continue the journey, quenching their desire to learn more about each character. Once again, powerful fiction at its best that adds dimension to the characters we love and loathe.

Please enjoy reading every line as much as she enjoyed writing them for all of us. Visit the author's website: robinalieberman.com

Author's Statement:

"There's a fire in all of us. We own it, control it, and must protect it from others who try to diminish it."

9 798985 629859